**Eliza[illegible] eyes widened as Rogan strode forcefully across the kitchen towards her. 'What are you doing?' she gasped, even as she took a wary step backwards.**

Rogan's mouth twisted with satisfaction as that step brought Elizabeth up against one of the kitchen cupboards, leaving her with nowhere else to go. 'I'm going to seduce you, of course,' he told her, standing so close to her that he could see the nerve pulsing erratically in her throat and the wide apprehension in her eyes. Could feel the heat of her body only inches away from his own. Smell the perfume that was uniquely Elizabeth's.

She blinked nervously. 'Rogan—'

'Elizabeth,' he murmured throatily, his gaze easily holding her wary one as he slowly lowered his head.

**Carole Mortimer** was born in England, the youngest of three children. She began writing in 1978, and has now written over one hundred and forty books for Mills & Boon. Carole has four sons—Matthew, Joshua, Timothy and Peter—and a bearded collie called Merlyn. She says, 'I'm happily married to Peter senior; we're best friends as well as lovers, which is probably the best recipe for a successful relationship.'

# THE MASTER'S MISTRESS

BY

CAROLE MORTIMER

First published in Great Britain 2010
Harlequin Mills & Boon Limited,
Eton House, 18-24 Paradise Road, Richmond, Surrey TW9 1SR



ISBN: 978 0 263 87774 8

Harlequin Mills & Boon policy is to use papers that are natural, renewable and recyclable products and made from wood grown in sustainable forests. The logging and manufacturing process conform to the legal environmental regulations of the country of origin.

Printed and bound in Spain
by Litografia Rosés, S.A., Barcelona

# THE MASTER'S MISTRESS

# CHAPTER ONE

*'...HE STOOD in the shadows of the night. Dark. Dangerous. A lethal predator. Glittering black eyes stared in at the woman through the window as she moved about the bedroom wearing only a towel draped about her silken nakedness. A slight smile curved her lips and she remained completely unaware of the danger that lay in wait for her outside in the darkness.'*

Elizabeth felt a shiver down her spine as she looked up from the book she was reading to her own bedroom window, wishing now that she had thought to draw the curtains before getting into bed. Except, like the woman in the story, Elizabeth had believed no one would be able to see into the second storey bedroom window of this remote house, perched high on the rugged Cornish cliffs. The tide must be in, covering the sandy beach, Elizabeth realised as she heard the roughness of the sea pounding against the cliffs.

She repressed another shiver before reading the next paragraph of her book.

*'Shoulder-length dark hair framed a face of hard, sensual magnetism. Those intense black eyes focused on the long creamy column of the woman's exposed throat and he could see the blood pulsing hotly through her veins. He possessed harshly hewn cheeks, a fierce slash of a nose, and chiselled lips that now drew back in a hiss to reveal elongated incisors as the woman dropped the towel to reveal the naked perfection of her body—'*

Crash!

So intent had Elizabeth been on the description of the sexy predator stalking the heroine that the sound of glass breaking somewhere downstairs made her gasp out loud, even as her fingers tightened about the book that had already succeeded in frightening the life out of her without this added scare!

What the devil *was* that?

Not a good choice of words, Elizabeth admonished herself shakily as she clutched the book to her before slowly sliding out from beneath the bedcovers.

There was something—or some*one*—downstairs!

More than likely someone. Elizabeth didn't believe for a moment that her own intruder was a real live vampire; the reason she enjoyed books like *Dangerous as the Night* was because she knew that the night monsters and predators in these stories were totally fictional.

No, the intruder wasn't any monster or a demon. More likely a burglar. There had been several break-ins in the area recently, and no doubt every burglar within a twenty-mile radius was aware by now that Brad Sullivan, the American owner of Sullivan House, had died of a heart attack almost a week ago.

What those burglars probably didn't know was that academic Dr Elizabeth Brown had arrived two weeks ago, employed for the summer to catalogue the books in the Sullivan library, and, because she didn't know what else to do until one of Brad's relatives arrived or contacted her, she was still in residence!

What should she do about the noise downstairs?

What *could* she do?

Mrs Baines, housekeeper at Sullivan House for the last twenty years, lived in a flat above the stable complex, to where she had disappeared once she had served Elizabeth her dinner and cleared away in the kitchen. Meaning the other woman probably had no idea that the main house had been broken into. There was no telephone extension in Elizabeth's bedroom, either, and she had stupidly left her mobile in the library earlier, on charge overnight.

Elizabeth's heart began to pound as she heard more muffled sounds from the floor below. It sounded like a voice muttering. A male voice, its tone impatiently aggressive.

Great. She couldn't just have a burglar break in; he had to be an angry one into the bargain!

Well, Elizabeth couldn't just stand here and wait for the man to come up the stairs in search of valuables, only to find her cowering under the duvet in one of the bedrooms, hoping not to be noticed. Burglar or not, she would have to go down and confront him. But obviously not without a weapon of some kind!

Tucking her book distractedly under her arm, Elizabeth moved stealthily across the bedroom to the door, opening it quietly to step out into the hallway, and pausing long enough to pick up the heavy brass ornament that stood on a table in the wide corridor. She made her way softly to the top of the stairs on the first floor so that she could look down into the huge reception hall. An eerie glow told her that someone had put a light on somewhere downstairs since she had gone up to bed half an hour or so ago.

Sullivan House was a three-storey mansion, originally built a couple of centuries ago for the head of some now defunct titled family, and several doors led off the marble-pillared reception hall. All of those doors remained firmly closed, with no visible light showing beneath them, not even a flashlight.

Elizabeth leant further over the polished oak banister, able to see now that the light was coming from the back of the house. The kitchen, most probably. Although what a burglar would find of value to steal in there, she had no idea; the only things that weren't integral parts of the kitchen were a microwave and an electric mixer. But there was also a set of sharp knives on top of one of the work surfaces, Elizabeth remembered in alarm. Any one of which could do serious damage to a person who dared to disturb the burglar!

Get a grip, Elizabeth, she instructed herself sternly, and she straightened her shoulders determinedly. There was no way she could cower and hide and hope that the burglar would just quickly take what he wanted and then go away. Whether she liked it or not—and she didn't!—Elizabeth had to confront the man and hope that her presence here would be enough to scare him off.

If it didn't…

She wasn't going to think about what would happen if the

situation backfired on her. She was an independent woman of twenty-eight. A university lecturer who had lived and worked in London for the last ten years. She seriously doubted a Cornish burglar would be half as dangerous as some of the strange people she was forced to share the tube with on a daily basis!

Had the wooden staircase always creaked like this? Elizabeth wondered in alarm as she began to descend it. She hadn't noticed it before, but she did now, as every step she took seemed to make the stairs groan in an alarming way that might alert the burglar to her presence before she was ready to confront him!

'Damn and double damn!'

The curse came from inside the kitchen even as Elizabeth crept stealthily down the hallway and saw the door was slightly ajar, allowing her to look into the kitchen through the narrow crack between the hinges of the door. She pressed herself urgently back against the wall as a dark-clothed figure moved across the brightly lit room.

Of course the man was wearing dark clothing; didn't all burglars?

Elizabeth drew in a deep breath, the shaking fingers of her left hand tightening about the brass ornament even as she reached out with her right hand to push the kitchen door inwards. She stepped inside the room, her blue gaze intent as she quickly scanned the kitchen, looking for the location of the intruder.

'Who the hell are you?'

Elizabeth was so shocked to hear the harsh but melodic voice coming from behind her that as she turned the brass ornament slipped from between her fingers.

'*Ow*!'

Straight onto the burglar's foot, she realised, as the man turned his back on her to bend down and grasp the top of his boot, where the heavy ornament had obviously landed, with painful results, before dropping to the tiled floor and rolling well out of Elizabeth's reach.

She looked around for another weapon to defend herself with, and very quickly realised that the burglar stood between her and that block of sharp knives.

The book she had been reading! Elizabeth had forgotten it was still tucked under her arm, but she grabbed it now and proceeded to hit the man repeatedly over the head with it.

'What the—!' The man straightened and turned, before reaching out to grasp both of Elizabeth's wrists and hold her hands up and away from him, well out of hitting distance. 'Will you stop attacking me, woman?' he growled.

Elizabeth became very still, eyes wide as she stared up at him.

It was the man from the book she had been reading!

The same narrowed and glittering black eyes. The same shoulder-length, silky dark hair. The same harshly sculptured face; prominent cheekbones, a hard slash of a nose, chiselled lips set in a grim line, and a square, determined jaw. The same very tall and lithely muscled body, completely dressed in black…

The same predator?

For the first time in her life Elizabeth fainted…

'Well, that was certainly different!' Rogan drawled derisively, as the woman he had picked up in his arms and then carried to the sitting-room sofa finally began to stir and regain consciousness.

She was a tiny woman, probably aged in her late twenties, and a whole foot shorter than him at only a couple of inches over five feet. She had short, auburn spiky-styled hair, a creamy, heart-shaped face; delicate cheekbones, a short, straight nose, a full bow of a mouth, and a small pointed chin that could be raised determinedly if she felt so inclined. As it had been earlier, when she'd attacked him—first with a brass ornament and then with a book, of all things!

Her eyes, as they opened, were a deep sky-blue, and surrounded by the thickest, darkest lashes Rogan had ever seen, he discovered as she sat up abruptly on the sofa to look across at him with the apprehension of a startled deer.

'Why are you still here?' she breathed warily.

'Why am I still here?' he repeated incredulously.

The woman moistened dry lips. 'You had plenty of time to get away when I—when I…'

'Swooned?' Rogan suggested mockingly.

'Fainted!' A dark frown appeared between those blue eyes. 'A perfectly normal reaction to being attacked by a burglar!'

Yes, that chin could definitely be very determined when this woman wished it to be! The bristling stance of that slender body beneath her slightly over-large cotton pyjamas also attested to her indignation.

Rogan had never particularly cared for the idea of women wearing pyjamas, preferring the woman in his bed to wear either nothing at all or something feminine in silk. Except this woman somehow managed to wear unflattering blue cotton pyjamas and still look sexy!

Maybe it was the way the material only hinted at the

curves beneath? Or could it be that the pale blue material made her eyes look bigger and bluer? Whatever it was, his little attacker was one very sexy package.

So what she was doing at Sullivan House?

His mouth tightened slightly. 'Perfectly natural,' he acknowledged. 'Except for two things. Firstly,' he bit out harshly as she raised questioning brows, 'I'm not a burglar. Secondly,' he continued, when she would have interrupted him, '*you* were the one doing the attacking. As evidenced by my bruised foot and battered head!'

Elizabeth felt the warm colour in her cheeks. She *had* attacked him. Firstly by dropping the ornament on his foot, and then by hitting him with the book.

The same book that now lay open across one muscled, denim-clad thigh! As if he had been reading it while waiting for Elizabeth to regain consciousness. Oh, good grief…!

Her chin rose defensively. 'I very much doubt that the police will be too interested in my efforts to defend myself considering that *you're* the one who broke in!'

'I wouldn't be too sure about that,' the man taunted. 'I've seen several cases in the English newspapers recently where the burglar was given compensation for being attacked by the owner of the house he had just broken into.'

Elizabeth had seen the same newspaper reports—and she questioned the sanity of the legal system!

'There's also the fact,' the man continued relentlessly, 'that I *didn't* break in.'

'You—'

'I unlocked the door into the kitchen by using the key from under the third flowerpot to the left on the windowsill outside,' he explained.

*What* key under the third flowerpot to the left on the windowsill outside? More to the point, how had this man known there was a key under that particular flowerpot in the first place?

'Have you been watching the house?' she gasped accusingly.

'Casing the joint, you mean?' he said scathingly.

'Yes!' Elizabeth glared at him indignantly, hating even the thought of someone—this man!—watching the recent daily comings and goings of the members of the household before attempting to break in.

'Interesting thought.' He nodded. 'This house is certainly remote enough; there isn't another house for miles. The spare key was conveniently left under a plant pot outside. No dog to bark at unusual noises in the night. In fact, no real security to talk of. At least none that's actually active at the moment.'

'How do you know that?' Elizabeth screeched. Not even the movement-sensor alarm in the house had been put on at night since Brad Sullivan had been rushed to hospital a week ago, as neither Mrs Baines nor Elizabeth knew how to set it.

'No flashing red light on the sensor.' He gave a pointed look at the monitor near the ceiling in the corner of the sitting room. 'Burglars have to be a bit more high-tech these days.' He shrugged dismissive shoulders beneath a thin black sweater.

Elizabeth's mouth tightened. 'Are you going to leave quietly and empty handed? Or do you intend to wait until the police arrive? I called them before coming downstairs,' she added defiantly as he raised dark, questioning brows.

'Did you?'

'Yes!'

She was a plucky little thing; Rogan would give her that.

She showed a lot of courage in the face of adversity. Although he very much doubted that a real burglar would have stopped to chat like this, let alone bothered to carry a woman to the sitting room after she had fainted!

He gave her a considering look. 'Did you know that when you lie you tend to bunch your left hand into a fist?'

'I do no—' She broke off her protest to stare down at her clenched fist, carefully unclenching it before adding, 'I *did* call the police, and they will be arriving any minute!'

Rogan relaxed back in his chair to place the ankle of one booted foot on top of his other black-denim-covered knee with a distinct lack of concern. 'That's going to be rather embarrassing for you,' he drawled ruefully.

Her eyes widened. 'For me?' she said. 'You're the one who broke in—'

'I used a key, remember?'

'Only because you knew it was under the plant pot!' she accused.

Rogan chuckled softly at her obvious indignation. 'Perhaps you ought to consider another reason than my having "cased the joint" to explain how I knew the key was there? It might also be an idea, when you go to bed at night, to read something a little less…' he picked up the book and read the first paragraph '…graphic, is probably the most polite description I can come up with!' He read the next paragraph. And the next. 'I had no idea that books about vampires could be so—'

'Give me that!' The fiery little redhead almost flew across the room to snatch the book out of his hand and thrust it behind her back, before glaring down at him. 'Are you going to leave now or not?'

Rogan mildly returned that fierce gaze. 'Not.'

She frowned her consternation at his reply. 'Surely you don't want to be arrested?'

He gave another shrug. 'That isn't going to happen any time soon.'

'When the police get here—'

'*If* the police get here,' he corrected pointedly, before continuing softly, 'I assure you they aren't going to arrest me.'

Elizabeth stared down at him in frustration, totally at a loss to know what to do or say next now that this man—no, this *burglar*!—actually refused to leave the house before the police got here. The fact that she'd had no telephone upstairs with which to call the police was irrelevant; he should have made good his escape long ago!

For the first time she noticed the blood-soaked paper towel wrapped about the palm of one long hard hand. 'How did you cut your hand if you didn't break a window to get in?' she pounced triumphantly.

He glanced down at his hand before looking back up at her. 'I dropped the damned milk bottle when I was getting it out of the fridge.' He scowled darkly. 'A piece of the glass pierced my hand when I got down on the floor to mop up the mess.'

That explained the crash Elizabeth had heard earlier.

Although not the reason this man had been taking a milk bottle from the fridge in the first place…

'You don't seriously expect me, or the police, to believe that explanation, do you?' she scorned.

Rogan had been travelling for hours. Fraught, tense hours, during which he hadn't been able to sleep. Consequently he was tired and still thirsty, and, amusing as this woman undoubtedly was, he was tired of answering her questions. Especially when for him there was still the more obvious question to be answered of what she was doing at Sullivan House at all!

He stood up, his expression becoming impatient as the redhead immediately took a step away from him. 'I would really rather drink a cup of the tea I was making earlier than your blood!'

'You were in the kitchen making a cup of tea?' she echoed incredulously.

Rogan raised dark brows. 'So?'

'So I don't— For your information, I read those sort of books purely for escapism!' she snapped defensively, as his earlier remark about not wanting to drink her blood suddenly registered with her.

Rogan smiled slightly. 'From the little I just read, I should think they might give you sexual inspiration, too!'

Her cheeks coloured bright red at his obvious mockery. 'Who *are* you?'

'Ah, at last a sensible question,' he murmured appreciatively, before turning to stroll from the room and return down the hallway to the kitchen, to lift the teapot and pour himself a cup of the dark liquid that was no doubt completely stewed by now.

So much for his intention of drinking a leisurely cup of tea before going upstairs and grabbing a decent night's sleep!

'Well?' The little firebrand had followed him to the kitchen and was now standing challengingly in the doorway.

Rogan took a sip of the tea before attempting to answer her. As he had suspected, it was slightly bitter. 'Well, what?' he snapped as he turned to refill the kettle before switching it on.

*'Who are you?'* she repeated forcefully.

His mouth twisted derisively. 'Obviously not a burglar!'

Elizabeth was very quickly coming to appreciate that fact. This man might look like every forbidden fantasy she had ever had, but a burglar wouldn't have stopped in the kitchen to make himself a cup of tea before stealing all the valuables! Or cleaned up the mess when a bottle of milk fell and smashed on the floor. Neither would he bother lifting a fainting female from that same floor in order to carry her to a comfortable sofa. And he certainly wouldn't enter into conversation about the book Elizabeth had been reading before she went to sleep…

How embarrassing was it that this man—a man whose every movement was as smoothly lethal as the predator hero in her book—had discovered her weakness for sexy vampire stories?

It wasn't just embarrassing—it was mortifying!

'Are you a relative of Mrs Baines?' Although what a relative of the housekeeper would be doing in the main house was beyond Elizabeth.

The intruder obviously thought the same thing, as he gave her a mocking glance before replying, 'Nope.'

'Are you going to tell me who you are, or—?'

'Or what?' He leant back against one of the work-units, arms folded across the broad width of that seriously muscled chest, those dark eyes narrowed on her ominously. 'I think a more interesting question to answer might be who are *you*?' he grated. 'More to the point, what the hell are you doing in Brad Sullivan's house?'

Elizabeth, momentarily mesmerised by the ripple of

muscle clearly shown beneath the man's tight black sweater, now recoiled as she heard the anger in his voice. 'I work here.'

'As what?'

Elizabeth wasn't sure she particularly cared for the insult that she detected in his tone. 'Not that it's any of your business, but my name is Elizabeth Brown, and I've been staying at Sullivan House so that I might catalogue Mr Sullivan's extensive library for him.'

'*You're* Dr E. Brown?' The man straightened, his dark gaze incredulous as it ran over Elizabeth from her head to her toes.

'That's correct, yes,' she confirmed guardedly, wondering why her name should mean anything to him. At the same time she felt incredibly warm under the intensity of his dark gaze.

'Dr Elizabeth Brown?'

She swallowed hard. 'Well…yes. It's an academic title rather than a medical one.' Why was she explaining herself to this man? What was it about him that compelled her to answer him? That made the very air about him seem to crackle with the force of his will?

'And here I was, expecting the good doctor to be a man,' the burglar-who-wasn't-a-burglar murmured, with a self-derisive shake of his head. 'Would that be the same Dr E. Brown who, a week ago, sent a next-day delivery letter to one Rogan Sullivan, at a PO Box in New York, to inform him that his father had suffered a heart attack and was seriously ill in hospital?'

Elizabeth gaped at him. There was no other word to describe it.

Dr Elizabeth Brown, respected university lecturer, most definitely gaped!

Surely the only way that this tall, dark and magnetically handsome man could know about that urgently sent letter would be if he was Rogan Sullivan himself?

The son of Brad Sullivan, who, as Mrs Baines had informed Elizabeth, hadn't been back to the family home in Cornwall for over fifteen years!

# CHAPTER TWO

'TEA...?' Rogan prompted mockingly as Elizabeth Brown—*Dr* Elizabeth Brown—moved dazedly across the kitchen to sit down on one of the breakfast stools, even while she continued to stare at him with a frown on her face.

She probably had to sit down before she fell down, Rogan acknowledged ruefully. No doubt it had been unnerving earlier, for this woman to suddenly hear someone banging and crashing about the kitchen and believing it to be a burglar. Only to now discover it was Brad Sullivan's long-lost son come to visit. A very short visit, if Rogan had his way.

'Tea would be...lovely,' she accepted. 'Um... Did you also receive the second letter I sent you?'

'Nope,' Rogan said shortly.

'Oh.'

Rogan's mouth twisted as he took pity on her dismayed expression. 'I know my father died, Elizabeth.'

How could Elizabeth have missed the fact that this man talked with an American accent? Probably because she had been too captivated by those deep and melodious tones to notice!

If she hadn't been so mesmerised then she might have

added two and two together and realised this man was probably related to Brad Sullivan. That he was, in fact, Brad Sullivan's son…

'Don't look for any physical resemblance between Brad and me,' Rogan Sullivan rasped harshly, the bitterness of his tone unmistakable. 'Or any other resemblance, for that matter. There isn't one, thank God!'

'I was just thinking what a pity it was that you had to learn of your father's death from a hospital official,' she said defensively.

He grimaced. 'I haven't been to the hospital. I did call, but they refused to give out any information on Brad's condition over the telephone. Luckily his lawyer was more forthcoming,' he added. 'About Brad's death *and* the instructions he gave him to arrange the funeral.'

Elizabeth gave a pained wince at this reminder that the funeral was arranged for three days' time. 'I'm really sorry your father died before you were able to get here.'

'Are you?'

'Of course.' She frowned at his sceptical tone.

'From what I can gather from his lawyer, Brad knew exactly how ill he was, and had been living on borrowed time for some years,' Rogan Sullivan revealed.

Borrowed time that Brad Sullivan had obviously chosen not to inform his only son about…

An only son who, Elizabeth now realised, was looking at her with far too much familiarity. That warm chocolate gaze moved slowly over her pyjama-clad body, pausing on the firm thrust of her breasts against the thin cotton material.

Elizabeth moved uncomfortably as she felt that gaze like a lick of heat across her skin. 'Would you excuse me for a few moments? If we're going to continue this conversation I would like to go upstairs and collect a robe,' she added pointedly, as Rogan Sullivan raised questioning brows.

'Oh, we're going to continue it,' he confirmed. 'And isn't it a little late for modesty?'

Elizabeth's cheeks coloured warmly as she stood up, thinking of being carried in this man's strong arms wearing nothing more than a pair of thin cotton pyjamas… 'Nevertheless, I believe I would feel more comfortable in my robe,' she said firmly.

'Fine,' Rogan accepted uninterestedly and he turned away, pretty sure that the good doctor was going upstairs in order to regroup as much as anything else.

She certainly looked more comfortable when she returned a few minutes later, wearing a serviceable blue and white striped robe tied neatly at the waist over those cotton pyjamas. Obviously Dr E. Brown was an altogether no-nonsense sort of woman. Not his father's type, he would have thought…

Rogan placed two fresh mugs of tea down forcefully onto the breakfast bar, before sitting on the stool opposite Elizabeth Brown's to regard her with narrowed, assessing eyes.

She straightened, obviously extremely uncomfortable. 'I thought that you might have telephoned once you had received my letter…'

He gave a humourless smile. 'Your very businesslike letter, informing me that "Mr Sullivan has suffered a heart attack"?' Rogan already regretted the impulse that had made him jump on a plane and fly to England, even though he had already known his father was dead, without having the prim Dr Elizabeth Brown pointing out the futility of his actions!

Had her letter had been businesslike? Elizabeth worried. Perhaps, she acknowledged with an inner grimace. But she hadn't known Brad Sullivan very well, and knew his son not at all, and, considering the obvious lack of warmth in their relationship, she had found it a very difficult letter to write. She could maybe have signed it with something a little less formal than 'Dr E. Brown', though…

Elizabeth had suggested that it might be better if Mrs Baines wrote the letter to Rogan Sullivan, but, faced with the housekeeper's almost hysterical distress after Brad's initial collapse, Elizabeth hadn't liked to press the point.

'I'm sorry if you found my letter a little—formal.' She picked up the mug of tea and took a reviving sip, some of the colour returning to her cheeks. 'Although it may have been more convenient if you had telephoned Mrs Baines to let her know of your imminent arrival. There have been several burglaries in the area recently, and if we had been expecting you I wouldn't have attacked you!' she added, slightly accusingly.

Elizabeth Brown was now embarrassed by her earlier behaviour, Rogan guessed easily. Not that she had any reason to be. His decision to come to England, after talking to his father's lawyer, had been a purely gut reaction. A need to see for himself that his father really was dead.

Consequently, Rogan hadn't thought to let anyone know of his arrival. Mrs Baines would have recognised him instantly, of course, despite the fact that he hadn't so much as been back to Sullivan House once for the last fifteen years, but there was no reason why Elizabeth Brown should have done so.

All the same, that embarrassed colour in the good doctor's cheeks was rather attractive, making her eyes appear a deeper, more sparkling blue. Embarrassment, no doubt, at having made such a monumental error as to accuse the son of the house of being a burglar!

Well, she needn't worry on that score. Rogan hadn't considered himself as the son of the house for years. The ten years he had spent in the American army had given him a new family. One he could depend on a damn sight more than the one he had been born into!

He gave a dismissive shrug. 'Forget it. It isn't important.'

Maybe not to him, Elizabeth accepted. But if she had known of Rogan's imminent arrival it might have saved her from embarrassing herself in that ridiculous way. And there was no way she could forget she had attacked him with a book, of all things. The brass ornament dropping on his foot had probably left a bruise too, despite the heavy black boots he was wearing.

Elizabeth looked across at him with new, assessing eyes. Rogan had been right when he'd claimed he bore no resemblance to his father, in looks or nature.

Brad Sullivan's hair had been blond and thinning, his eyes a steely blue, and although he might once have been as tall and muscular as his son, the older man had been painfully thin and slightly stooped before his death. Not even the facial bone structure was the same: Brad's face had been more rounded, where Rogan Sullivan's was all harshly sculptured angles.

All harshly sculptured extremely handsome angles…

Rogan Sullivan really did resemble those darkly dangerous and sexy heroes who so often appeared in the vampire and demon books Elizabeth read for relaxation after spending her days and evenings totally immersed in teaching history to university students. No excuse, she admitted, but she enjoyed reading those types of books because of their complete escapism. She certainly hadn't appreciated having this man taunt her about them!

This man who had so far shown remarkably little emotion over his father's recent death…

Mrs Baines had briefly explained the situation between father and son to her; Brad and Rogan Sullivan had argued after the death of Rogan's mother, Brad's wife, Maggie, fifteen years ago, when Rogan had been aged only eighteen. Rogan had apparently left home shortly after that, and the next time his father had heard from him it had been to learn he had returned to his native America and joined the army.

Not that Elizabeth had needed to be told that the relationship was a strained one after learning that Brad's only way of contacting his only child was through a post office box in New York!

'Don't presume to make judgements based on things you can't possibly understand,' Rogan advised as he saw the emotions flickering across Elizabeth Brown's expressive face: curiosity, quickly followed by a faintly disapproving curl of that sensually fuller top lip.

She arched auburn brows. 'I wasn't aware I was doing so.'

'No?'

'No.' She frowned her irritation with the challenge.

Rogan gave a humourless smile. 'You were sitting there thinking that I don't seem very upset for someone whose father has just died!'

That was *exactly* what Elizabeth had been thinking!

But perhaps she was misjudging Rogan? After all, she had no idea why father and son had argued only months after the death of Rogan's mother, followed by long years of estrangement. For all she knew Brad could have been a terrible husband and father.

Much like her own…

Except it was all too easy, now that the politely charming Brad was dead, to blame the mocking and seemingly uncaring Rogan Sullivan for the strained relationship that had existed between father and son.

'So, what are you doing here?' Those dark eyes were hard as onyx as Rogan Sullivan looked across at her in an uncomfortably assessing manner.

Elizabeth frowned. 'I believe I already told you. I'm here to catalogue your father's library.'

'You said that, yeah…' he drawled. 'I meant what are you *still* doing here now that he's dead?'

'I didn't know what else to do,' Elizabeth admitted ruefully. 'Your father engaged my services for six weeks, and…' She shook her head. 'I didn't know what else to do,' she repeated lamely.

Those chiselled lips curled disdainfully. 'Do a lot of cataloguing, do you?'

'During the summer holidays, yes. Exactly what are you implying, Mr Sullivan?' Elizabeth demanded indignantly, as she saw speculation in those mocking eyes.

He shrugged. 'That maybe physical over-exertion could be the reason my father had a heart attack a week ago?'

Elizabeth gasped. 'Are you implying that I had a—a personal relationship with your *father*?'

'You tell me,' Rogan taunted; this woman really was very beautiful when she lost her temper!

Her eyes glittered deeply blue, and there was heated

colour in her cheeks. The fullness of her lips was set determinedly, her pointed chin was raised challengingly, and the spiky style of that red hair gave the overall impression of an indignant hedgehog!

'The library was here when we moved to England twenty years ago and my father bought this house; I don't recall him even considering having it catalogued before,' Rogan goaded deliberately.

A nerve pulsed in her stubbornly set jaw. 'And how would *you* know what your father may or may not have considered doing when the only contact you've had with him, for the last five years at least, has been through a PO Box?'

Rogan narrowed his eyes menacingly. 'I warned you not to speculate about things you don't understand, Liza.'

That angry colour drained as quickly from her cheeks as it had appeared. 'I prefer to be called Elizabeth or Dr Brown!' she bit out stiltedly.

Rogan eyed her consideringly. Obviously he had hit on a raw nerve of some kind by the shortening of her name. 'Okay, so don't speculate about things you don't understand…*Elizabeth*,' he conceded dryly.

What Elizabeth didn't understand was why she was responding to this man's taunts and insinuations at all!

As Dr Brown, highly qualified lecturer in history at one of the most prestigious universities in the country, she was held in deep respect by students and faculty colleagues alike. As Elizabeth Brown, a woman of considerable financial independence, she made a point of avoiding any and all situations that might lead to emotional confrontation of any kind. Especially with a man whose very presence unnerved her!

'Unlike you, I'm not so hot on formality,' Rogan said.

'My friends call me Rogue,' he explained, and Elizabeth gave a confused frown.

Rogue?

How fitting a name was that for this dangerously disturbing man!

'How lucky for me, then, that I don't happen to be one of your friends,' Elizabeth answered coolly. 'I would prefer to use Mr Sullivan, or Rogan if you insist on informality.'

'Oh, I do, Elizabeth, I most certainly do,' he murmured huskily.

She avoided meeting that warm and mocking dark gaze. 'Perhaps we should resume this conversation in the morning, Rogan? We don't seem to be achieving very much tonight.'

'Except being rude to each other,' Rogan pointed out.

'Exactly.' She nodded briskly. 'You are obviously tired after your journey—' She broke off as Rogan gave a chuckle, a disconcerted frown on her brow as she looked across at him questioningly. And she felt the lurch in her chest, the swelling of her breasts and tightening of her nipples, at the way the amusement in his face made him appear even more dangerous…

Appear dangerous? This man *was* dangerous! And he induced an awareness in Elizabeth, a physical arousal, that was totally alien to her.

'Nice cop-out, Elizabeth,' Rogan jeered, stretching wearily. 'But I'm afraid I'm always this outspoken—what's your excuse?'

It took all of Elizabeth's will-power to drag her gaze away from the flexing of those muscles in the broadness of Rogan Sullivan's shoulders. Even so, her nipples actually ached now, and there was an unaccustomed warmth between her thighs…

Her mouth firmed and she straightened suddenly. 'It's late, I was terrified out of my wits a short time ago, and I'm tired…'

'Terrified out of your wits?' he echoed incredulously, that dark gaze once again compelling. 'I'd hate to see what your response would be if you weren't so terrified!' He touched his temple pointedly, a slight redness of the skin showing where Elizabeth had struck him with her book.

A book whose predatory hero was no doubt going to seem very one-dimensional after she had come face to face with the very real—and very disturbing—flesh-and-blood man!

Elizabeth watched his long fingers as they ran lightly across his bruised flesh before pushing back the long length of his dark hair in a movement that seemed habitual. That hair looked as soft as silk. A silkiness Elizabeth longed to touch and thread her own fingers into before pulling his head down and—

She gathered herself up. 'No doubt you know which bedroom to use?' she bit out sharply.

'No doubt,' Rogan Sullivan drawled, those black eyes openly laughing at her.

Elizabeth had almost reached the kitchen door, almost made her dignified exit, and was congratulating herself on how well she had regrouped after physically attacking Rogan Sullivan in his own family home, when he made his own last mocking comment.

'Don't forget to get your book from the drawing room…'

She faltered slightly, her eyes closing briefly in embarrassment at this second taunting reminder of the book she had been reading earlier.

'The cover alone would be enough to shock Mrs Baines senseless, let alone its contents!' Rogan Sullivan added.

Elizabeth drew in a deep, controlling breath before she turned to glare across the room at him. 'I should put something on that cut on your hand, if I were you. It would be such a pity if it were to become infected. It might even result in lockjaw!' she added with saccharin sweetness.

'I can imagine how much that might bother you.' He gave an appreciative chuckle.

'You have no idea!' Elizabeth gave him one last scathing glance before sweeping out of the kitchen. Well, sweeping as much as she could when she was wearing a pair of blue cotton pyjamas and a striped bathrobe!

She paused long enough in the drawing room to take advantage of Rogan Sullivan's jeering advice concerning taking her book back upstairs with her.

All the time she was aware that any dreams or erotic fantasies she might have tonight would all be about a dark-haired, dark-eyed, dangerous man dressed completely in black.

A man known to his friends as Rogue…

'Mrs Baines seemed to be of the opinion that we would be eating breakfast together, and I didn't like to disappoint her,' Rogan said the following morning, as Elizabeth came to an abrupt halt in the doorway of the breakfast room the moment she saw he was already seated at the small table.

A slightly more officious-looking Elizabeth Brown than the night before; she wore a silky cream blouse tucked into black tailored trousers, with flat court shoes. That red hair was as perky and spiky as the previous evening, but she had added mascara to those already dark, sooty lashes, and a deep peach gloss to the fullness of her lips.

Officious, but still beautiful, Rogan decided approvingly

as he stood up to hold a chair for her to sit down after she had reluctantly entered the room. 'Just so that you know I *do* remember some of the manners my mother taught me all those years ago,' he bent to murmur derisively beside her left ear.

'I'm pleased to hear it!' Elizabeth ignored his close proximity and picked up her napkin. She placed it purposefully across her trouser-clad knees before continuing to ignore him as she looked over the contents of the table.

All the time she was completely aware of how devastatingly male Rogan looked, with that long dark hair still damp from the shower. He was wearing a black T-shirt that clearly defined his muscled chest and arms, with black combat trousers sitting low down on the leanness of his waist and emphasising the powerful length of his legs…

'Would you like me to pour you some coffee?' Rogan offered as he raised the cafetière invitingly, and in the process once again stood just a little too close to Elizabeth for comfort.

The feral grin he gave as Elizabeth shot him a slightly nervous glance told her that he was totally aware of the effect his close proximity was having on her equilibrium. That he'd already noted the flush in her cheeks, the way she couldn't seem to breathe properly, and the slight trembling of her hands.

How could she not be affected? Elizabeth accepted ruefully. Men like Rogan Sullivan—hard, tough, dangerous—were completely beyond her everyday acquaintance. The only males she usually met on a day-to-day basis were either other academics or students much younger than herself.

She occasionally accepted an innocuous luncheon or dinner invitation from one of her male colleagues, but other than that Elizabeth preferred to keep her life uncomplicated by personal relationships. She had certainly never met anyone even remotely like Rogan before!

But she certainly wasn't so disconcerted by all this blatantly displayed testosterone that she was willing to forego her morning cup of coffee because of it! 'Thank you,' she accepted, with a dismissive glance in his direction.

Mistake!

As she had known she would, Elizabeth had dreamt about this man last night. Once she had finally managed to fall asleep at all, that was. Intense, disturbing dreams that had included fulfilling the fantasy she'd had last night of running her fingers through that over-long dark hair, before moving lower to caress the width of those muscled shoulders and down the hardness of his back. In her dream she had also caressed other places she would really rather not think about right now!

But the reality of the man was so much more disturbing than any dream. He simply oozed hard masculinity from every pore in his muscled body, from that hewn and ruggedly handsome face to the strength of his perfectly toned body. He even smelt male, his aftershave sharp and tangy, with a hint of spice that tantalised the senses almost as much as the man did himself.

He knew it too, and was perfectly comfortable with all that blatant masculinity, Elizabeth acknowledged slightly resentfully. 'Are you expecting to suddenly have to go into combat here in the wilds of Cornwall?' she taunted, with a scathing glance at the dark clothing and heavy black boots he seemed to favour wearing.

He shrugged. 'I just threw a few things into a holdall after receiving your letter. Besides, I find it's always best to be prepared.' Rogan eyed her mockingly as he resumed his seat opposite her at the intimately small table. 'After all, one never knows when and where one might be attacked!'

Warm colour entered those slightly hollow cheeks at the deliberateness of Rogan's taunt. 'Mrs Baines mentioned you left the army five years ago?' She obviously chose to take his taunt at face value.

'Yes,' he confirmed evenly.

'What career do you have now?'

'I keep busy with this and that.'

'What sort of this and that?'

Rogan narrowed his gaze darkly. 'You're very nosy for someone who supposedly only came here to catalogue my father's library for him.'

'There's no "supposedly" about it,' she assured primly. 'I was merely attempting to make conversation.'

'Make it about something else,' he bit out curtly.

Rogan didn't discuss the work he did. With anyone. Least of all a woman he had only met eight hours ago.

Although it was starting to seem much longer than that…

'If I'm nosy, then you're completely lacking in manners!' She frowned at his rudeness.

Rogan gave an uninterested shrug. 'What else did you expect from a man whose father's only means of contacting him was through a PO Box!'

A nerve pulsed in her cheek. 'I wasn't meaning to be rude when I made that comment.'

'Weren't you?' Rogan asked knowingly.

Okay, yes, she had been, Elizabeth accepted guiltily. Which was a little unfair of her when she really knew nothing about their family situation. When this man's father had just died…

'What about you, Elizabeth?' Rogan Sullivan arched a dark brow in query. 'What does Dr E. Brown do when she isn't cataloguing someone's library?'

'She teaches. History. At a London university,' she expanded as he seemed to be expecting more.

'Wow.'

'It's a subject I happen to love.' She bristled defensively at the obvious lack of enthusiasm in his voice.

'You're comfortable with things that have already happened rather than those that haven't?'

Elizabeth had never thought of it in that particular way before... 'Is there something wrong with that?' she asked.

A shrug stretched the black material of his T-shirt tighter across the wide width of his shoulders. 'Not at all. Except a life with no surprises must be...'

'Comfortable?' Elizabeth supplied tersely.

'Boring,' Rogan Sullivan finished with an unrepentant grin, his teeth very white and even against that lightly bronzed skin.

'That happens to be the way I prefer it.' She stood up abruptly. 'With your permission, I think I'll take my coffee with me into the library and get started on some work.'

Dark brows rose teasingly. 'With my permission?' he echoed.

It had occurred to Elizabeth shortly before she'd fallen asleep the night before that with Brad Sullivan's death, if she stayed on here as originally planned, she would now effectively be working for Rogan...

She nodded tersely. 'Unless you would prefer me to stop working on cataloguing the books?'

'I—' Rogan's attention turned to the doorway as he saw Mrs Baines standing there hesitantly.

'I wondered if I could get either of you something hot for breakfast?' the elderly housekeeper offered huskily, the strain of the last few days evident in the paleness of her cheeks and the slight redness of her eyes.

'Elizabeth?' Rogan prompted crisply.

'Not for me, thanks.' She gave the older woman a regretful smile.

'Or me,' Rogan said. 'We'll both be finished in here in a few minutes, if you want to clear away then,' he assured Mrs Baines lightly, having only vague memories of the sixty-year-old widow who had moved to Sullivan House with a sixteen-year-old son twenty years ago.

He leant back in his chair to look at Elizabeth with enigmatic dark eyes once they were alone again, arms now folded across that wide, muscled chest. 'So, have you found any priceless treasures in the library yet?' he wanted to know.

'One or two, yes.' She nodded. 'A first edition of Charles Darwin's *Origin of the Species* alone is worth a considerable amount of money.'

His brows rose. 'How much money?'

'Probably several hundred thousand pounds. And there are several others: a couple of Dickenses and a Chaucer. They're also very collectible.'

'I'm really not that interested, Elizabeth,' Rogan rasped.

Her cheeks became flushed. 'Then why bother to ask?'

He gave a shrug. 'It seemed like a good idea at the time.'

'And is your interest usually this fleeting?'

A slow smile curved those sculptured lips even as the dark eyes once again openly laughed at her. 'It depends what that interest happens to be…'

There was no mistaking the deliberate innuendo in

Rogan's tone. Nor Elizabeth's longing to wipe that smile from his ruggedly handsome face!

What was it about Rogan Sullivan that brought out these uncharacteristic feelings of violence in her? That caused her to be constantly antagonised by him?

The answer to that was easy! Everything about him made her feel defensive, while at the same time making her feel vulnerable and very feminine in a way that was totally unfamiliar to her. As well as uncomfortable…

Elizabeth Brown was defensive, nosy and confrontational, Rogan recognised as he continued to look at her admiringly from between narrowed lids. An interesting combination for a university lecturer in History who read steamy vampire novels when she was alone in bed at night and didn't like surprises in her personal life.

Whereas Rogan was an adrenaline junkie who lived for the challenges in his own life, personal and otherwise!

Elizabeth's mouth firmed. 'Obviously your…*interest* doesn't lie in rare books.'

'Obviously not,' Rogan agreed, inwardly starting to regret deliberately baiting her.

She *had* arrived two weeks ago to catalogue Brad's library—Rogan had checked that out with Mrs Baines earlier—and, pleasurable as it might be, he shouldn't be taking out his present frustration with the situation he found himself in on her.

Because his father's sudden death had completely removed any possibility of the two men ever coming to any sort of understanding…

The two Sullivan men had never had the easiest of relationships. When the family had lived in the States Brad had owned and run one of the most prestigious advertising companies in New York, and his hours of work had been long and frantic. The family home had been in the suburbs, often meaning that Brad had spent weekday nights at the apartment he'd kept in the city. Not much had changed after the family had moved to England twenty years ago, so his father could open an office there. Brad had stayed in London during the week, only returning to Sullivan House for the weekends.

Consequently Brad hadn't been around much, and had never attended any of the school events to which parents were invited—meaning Rogan's mother, the Irish/American Maggie, had been the one to attend rugby matches, sports days, and the school plays in which Rogan had appeared.

Maggie had always been the bridge between Rogan and Brad, and when she had died so unexpectedly the two men had found they had absolutely nothing in common. Added to which, Brad had been furious when Rogan had refused to take up his place at Oxford University and instead returned to America and joined the army there.

Rogan straightened abruptly. 'Continue to catalogue the library, by all means,' he said brusquely. 'Whoever inherits will no doubt consider selling them if some of the books are as valuable as you say they are.'

Elizabeth's eyes widened. 'You aren't expecting that to be you?'

Rogan Sullivan's laugh lacked all humour. 'I have an appointment with Desmond Taylor, Brad's lawyer, later this morning, so no doubt all will be revealed then. But I'd think it doubtful, wouldn't you?'

Elizabeth no longer knew what to think. About this situation. Or, indeed, about Rogan Sullivan…

# CHAPTER THREE

'THIS is very kind of you,' Rogan said as he sat beside Elizabeth as she drove her Mini Cooper into town.

Elizabeth briefly turned her attention from driving along the narrow coast road to shoot him a narrow-eyed glance.

Kindness on her part had nothing to do with the two of them being here together. How could it, when Rogan had more or less commandeered both Elizabeth and her car so that he might keep his appointment in town this morning with Desmond Taylor, his father's lawyer?

Having flown into England late the previous night, and feeling tired after a long flight, it appeared that instead of hiring a car Rogan had simply got in a taxi and asked the driver to take him to Sullivan House. Consequently, he had no transport of his own.

As Elizabeth now worked for him—for the moment at least—Rogan had very generously given her permission to take a couple of hours off so that she could drive him into town!

'Don't push your luck,' she warned him tersely.

He arched dark brows. 'Is that what I'm doing?'

'You know you are.' Elizabeth's only consolation in being coerced in this way was that her car was obviously too small for a broadly muscled man of well over six feet in height. It was extremely unlikely that Rogan was at all comfortable in the passenger seat! Although his close proximity—those muscled arms and long, powerful legs were only inches from her own—was a little disturbing, to say the least…

Rogan glanced out of the side window, down the cliffs to where the sea was currently lapping gently onto the golden sand. 'I'd forgotten how ruggedly beautiful it is here…'

'I expect it's a lot different from New York?'

'Yes.' Except Rogan wasn't always in New York…

He didn't really live anywhere on a permanent basis, was never in one place long enough to put down any roots. Anyone important who needed to get in contact with him urgently had his private mobile number. Anyone else could use the PO Box.

Including his father.

Rogan had no idea yet how he felt about his father's death; he was still coming to terms with the finality of it. Dealing with emotions had never been Rogan's strong point—especially when those emotions were so ambivalent.

Although he sensed that Elizabeth Brown disapproved of his reticence on the subject.

Well, she would just have to go on disapproving!

Rogan would deal with his father's death in the same way he dealt with everything. Alone. He had been alone for so long now that he simply didn't know how to be any other way. Didn't want to know, either.

'I shouldn't be too long,' he told Elizabeth once she had parked the Mini and he could at last uncurl his cramped body from inside the small confines of the car.

'Take your time,' she answered distractedly. 'I have a little personal shopping to do anyway.'

'Fine.' He nodded. 'I suggest we meet back under the clock-tower here in the square in an hour or so, and then find somewhere to have lunch.'

'Lunch?' Elizabeth echoed sharply, and she straightened so suddenly from locking the car that her head briefly swam.

'Lunch,' Rogan reiterated firmly. 'We're in town anyway, and it'll be almost lunchtime, so why not?'

Why not? Because Elizabeth didn't *want* to have lunch with this compelling and disturbing man. In fact, she was quickly coming to realise that she wanted as little to do with Rogan Sullivan as humanly possible!

Not an easy thing to do when for the moment, they were actually staying in the same house…

'Okay, lunch in an hour,' she conceded.

'Or so,' Rogan added.

'Whatever.' Elizabeth gave him one last impatient glance before turning away to walk determinedly towards the shops on the other side of the square.

'Just make sure he stays put,' Rogan snapped into his mobile as he strode restlessly up and down in front of the clock-tower, waiting for Elizabeth to rejoin him so they could have lunch together.

'That's easier said than done, Rogue—'

'Just *do* it!' Rogan growled, turning to pace back the other way and instantly finding himself face to face with a pale and wide-eyed Elizabeth Brown. 'Later, Ace,' he said curtly, before ending the call and dropping his mobile into the back pocket of the black denims he had changed into before coming out.

'I— Did your meeting go well?'

Rogan gave a hard smile. 'It would appear that I'm my father's heir after all, if that's what you're asking.'

Colour heightened Elizabeth Brown's cheeks. 'It wasn't.'

'No?' he jeered.

'No.' She frowned. 'It's really none of my business, is it?'

'No, it isn't,' Rogan agreed. In truth, he was surprised—considering the state of their relationship the last fifteen years—that his father had decided to leave everything to him after all. But maybe Brad had considered a dogs' home—which had probably been his only alternative—slightly less appealing than his own son! 'Nevertheless, I'm sure you have an opinion on the subject!'

Elizabeth was having to force herself to concentrate on what Rogan was saying. Not easy after overhearing his end of the telephone conversation with someone called Ace!

*Just make sure he stays put...*

She frowned as she remembered the implacable tone of voice he'd used towards the other man. Rogan was obviously not a man it would be wise to cross!

Or be attracted to...

Unfortunately, Elizabeth suspected it was already too late to warn herself off being attracted to Rogan. Just looking at him sent shivers of awareness up and down her spine. That over-long dark hair. Those dark and piercing eyes. The firm sensuality of his mouth. The lean sensitivity of his hands. The leashed power in that perfectly muscled body...

'No doubt you have one of those perfect families?' Rogan Sullivan continued scathingly. 'Perfect mother. Perfect father. Perfect everything.'

He had no idea! Elizabeth's family had to be even more dysfunctional than his own!

'Come on, Liza—'

'I believe I told you I prefer to be called Elizabeth!' Her eyes flashed with sudden anger. Her father had always called her Liza, and she certainly wanted no reminders of him.

Rogan glanced at her, irritated with himself because of how attractive he found the way the colour came and went in her cheeks, and the way her eyes sparkled with emotion when she was angry or annoyed—

Whoa!

Elizabeth Brown wasn't his type. At all. Rogan preferred his women to be tall, soft and feminine. Women who knew and accepted that a relationship with him had no future. He wanted nothing to do with a woman who was short and prickly, a university lecturer immersed up to her pretty neck in history, whose ideal was no doubt the house with the picket fence and two point four children!

All the same, Rogan couldn't stop himself from flirting with her just a little, to see how uncomfortable—and beautiful—it made her. He deliberately took a step closer, crowding her. 'Liza is so much more—friendly, don't you think…?' he murmured huskily.

Those deep blue eyes narrowed to warning slits. 'I have no wish to be friendly with a man who can speak to people like you just did on your phone,' she said scornfully.

Rogan's eyes widened. So Dr Elizabeth Brown had overheard part of his conversation with Ace, had she? And she'd obviously drawn her own conclusions from it too. No doubt helped along by an over-active imagination from reading too many vampire books!

Well, Rogan had ceased even trying to explain himself a long time ago—least of all to a woman as unbending as this one. 'What can I say?' He gave an unconcerned shrug. 'Sometimes a little aggression is necessary when people won't do as they're told the first time.'

Elizabeth repressed a shudder of apprehension at the callousness of his tone. Her first impression of this man last night had been the correct one after all; he really was dangerous!

'Don't look so worried, Elizabeth,' Rogan Sullivan murmured softly. 'The only time I enjoy hearing a woman scream is in bed…'

The erotic images that statement instantly conjured into Elizabeth's head, of a lithe, bronzed and naked body entwined with a much paler and softer one, caused the colour to once again burn hotly in her cheeks.

She turned away. 'Perhaps we should get back to Sullivan House after all.'

'Running scared, Elizabeth?'

'Of *you*?' Her eyes glittered as she glared at him. 'I hardly think so!'

'You could have fooled me!' Rogan gave her another one of those mocking smiles. 'We're only going to have lunch, Elizabeth, we're not going out on a date together.'

She hadn't imagined for one moment that their lunch together could be called a date. It was just a little disconcerting—more than a little, if she were brutally honest with herself—to think of spending time alone in a restaurant with a man who was so blatantly, breathtakingly male that just looking at him made even her teeth ache in awareness!

It was a raw attraction that was completely corroborated at that moment, as a woman passing by on the pavement happened to glance casually their way—only for her attention to suddenly become riveted on Rogan, a flush warming her cheeks as he shot her a lazy smile.

Rogan Sullivan wasn't just dangerous—he was utterly lethal!

Elizabeth scowled. 'I'm not hungry after all,' she snapped. 'It must be all that aggressive talk earlier on—you're nothing but a bully!' she added challengingly.

Rogan looked at her rigidly disapproving face and chose not to explain his firm orders to Ace about making sure Ricky stayed put—after all, Ricky didn't know what was good for him.

'Hasn't affected *my* appetite,' Rogan assured her blithely, giving her no more opportunity to disagree with him as he took a firm hold of her arm and strode forcefully towards the Bell and Sceptre Hotel, across the other side of the square.

'So, what shall we talk about?' Elizabeth said dryly to Rogan once they were seated at a table in the saloon bar of the hotel where he had decided they were having lunch.

He sat back against the bench seat, seemingly unaware of the interested female stares that had been coming his way ever since he had gone up to the crowded bar to order their food.

Including Elizabeth's own more surreptitious glances!

Had she ever been this physically aware of a man before? Not that she could remember. But she was so aware of Rogan, on so many levels, that she felt she could see and hear practically nothing else but him. Her skin felt hotter than the temperature in the bar warranted. Her breasts were swollen, the nipples slightly tingly, and there was a telling dampness between her thighs that shocked her…

Ridiculous. From the little Elizabeth had overheard of his telephone conversation with someone called Ace, Rogan Sullivan was little more than a thug. No doubt his years in the army, the physical discipline he had learnt there, had made him as lethal as any of the weapons he had been trained to use.

As a woman who had always valued intellect rather than muscle, how could Elizabeth possibly find all that leashed physical power arousing? Except…she did! To such an extent that she could imagine nothing more pleasurable than ripping all that black clothing from Rogan's bronzed and muscular body so that she might caress every powerful, rugged inch of him.

In fact, just thinking about doing those things increased the temperature of her own body to an almost unbearable degree!

Rogan gave a dismissive shrug. 'Who says we have to talk at all? I came here for food, not conversation.'

Elizabeth frowned even as she sat back to allow the barmaid to place their plates of food on the table. A young and pretty barmaid, who could no more take her eyes off Rogan Sullivan, as she laid out their knives and forks, than the woman in the square had a few minutes ago.

'Thanks.' Rogan gave the young girl the same lazy grin that had so enthralled the woman in the square earlier.

Elizabeth shot him a scathing glance as that grin once again caused a slightly flustered response, but in the young barmaid this time. Really, this man ought to come with a 'danger' label attached!

'What?' he prompted irritably, once he and Elizabeth were alone again and he looked up to see her disgusted expression.

Elizabeth gave a slight shake of her head. 'Just deploring my own gender for their obvious gullibility to a sexy smile!'

He raised speculative brows. 'You think I have a sexy smile?'

She frowned her irritation. 'I didn't say that—'

'Yeah, you did.'

Yes, she had, Elizabeth acknowledged with an inner groan. Damn the man! She sat forward to pick up her knife and fork in preparation for eating the chicken salad that was looking less and less appetising as this embarrassing conversation continued. 'You probably practise in front of a mirror for hours just to get that effect,' she said, in an effort to puncture his enormous ego.

Rogan gave an appreciative chuckle at her disgruntled accusation. 'Not true. I had no idea my smile was at all sexy until you said it was.'

'Could we just eat?' Elizabeth snapped.

Rogan grinned unabashedly at her obvious discomfort. 'If you think that you still can!'

Blue eyes shot sparks at him. 'You aren't my type, Mr Sullivan,' she said waspishly.

'Now, there's a challenge if ever I heard one…' Rogan mused.

Her eyes widened in alarm. 'It certainly wasn't meant as one!'

'Hmm…' Rogan speculated enigmatically, dark eyes narrowed. 'So what *is* your usual type, Elizabeth?' he asked, as he picked up his fork and began to eat the steak and ale pie he had ordered for his own lunch.

She avoided that probing gaze. 'I thought you preferred not to talk?'

'I've changed my mind.'

'Unfortunately for you, so have I!'

'Humour me, Elizabeth, hmm?' he encouraged softly.

Elizabeth didn't want to humour this man. In fact, she wished they had never started this conversation! Especially as she did find his smile sexy—as did every other woman who so much as looked at him!

Her chin rose defensively. 'If you must know, I prefer brain over brawn.'

He became very still. Watchfully, dangerously so. 'You think I'm just muscle and no brain?'

'I didn't say that—'

'As good as,' he bit out. 'What constitutes an intelligent man to you, Elizabeth?'

She grimaced. 'I didn't mean to sound insulting—'

'Oh, I think that you did,' Rogan grated harshly. 'Does a first-class degree in Computer Science and a doctorate in Computer Analysis pass as intelligent in your book?'

Elizabeth swallowed hard. 'I thought you had been in the army for most of the last fifteen years.'

'Where, if you're so inclined, they teach you to use your brain as well as how to shoot guns!' he assured her.

There was no mistaking the anger in Rogan's tone now. And rightly so. Somehow in the last fifteen years this man had achieved a first-class degree and a doctorate, for goodness' sake. Giving him the same right as Elizabeth to use the title of doctor if he so chose.

She gave an awkward grimace. 'I apologise if I sounded rude. But—'

'Let's just leave it at the apology, hmm, Elizabeth?' he advised in an off-hand manner. 'Any more insults from you and I'm likely to lose my appetite!'

Elizabeth already had lost *her* appetite. Completely. And

it wasn't all due to the last verbal exchange with Rogan. Some of it was due to the fascination of watching the lean strength of his hands as he ate his meal with silent efficiency, as if he needed the fuel it would provide rather than obtaining any real enjoyment from the food itself.

This was a man totally beyond Elizabeth's experience. An enigma, in fact. He looked rough, tough and quite frankly dangerous. But his degree and doctorate also proclaimed him to be a man of high intelligence. Something she should perhaps have realised *before* she insulted him…

She swallowed hard. 'I really am sorry if I sounded less than polite just now, Mr Sullivan.'

So he was back to being 'Mr Sullivan', was he? Rogan mused cynically. 'Don't give it another thought, *Elizabeth*,' he replied. 'You obviously can't help being insulting,' he added challengingly.

Her cheeks coloured attractively, making her hair appear redder and spikier. 'Now who's being rude?'

Rogan chuckled softly. 'It must be catching! Most people consider me something of a pussycat,' he teased.

'The lethal type that stalks in a jungle, perhaps?' Elizabeth said dryly.

'Perhaps,' he dismissed evenly; until he'd left the military five years ago, she would have been closer than she realised!

'So,' she went on. 'What is it you do, exactly, with your degree in Computer Science and your doctorate in Computer Analysis?'

'Analyse…?'

She gave a pained frown. 'I'm trying to make polite conversation, Mr Sullivan; you might at least try to reciprocate!'

'Why?'

'Because it's what people do!'

'Is it?' Rogan murmured. 'Perhaps if you were to start calling me Rogue instead of Mr Sullivan I might feel more inclined to reciprocate?'

She shifted uncomfortably. 'I agreed to use the name Rogan.'

'But not Rogue?' he taunted.

'No.' She grimaced.

'Fair enough.' Rogan leant back against the bench seat to look across at her through narrowed lids. 'You haven't eaten very much.' He frowned at her almost untouched plate.

'I told you, I'm not hungry.' She gave up any pretence of eating and pushed her plate away. 'I forgot to ask earlier how your hand is today,' she added politely.

'Are you offering to kiss it better?' Rogan responded mockingly, after glancing down at the already healing nick on the palm of his right hand. He had several scars on other parts of his body that would no doubt make this self-contained woman scream in horror at the thought of the violence behind them!

'I'm not your mother, Rogan!' Her eyes flashed with temper.

A temper Rogan was pretty sure this controlled woman was usually at pains to conceal. Interesting… 'No, I can definitely vouch for that,' he said dryly; the primly correct Elizabeth Brown was absolutely nothing like his gregarious Irish mother.

'Are you like her?' Elizabeth's curiosity had obviously got the better of her.

Rogan's mouth tightened. 'In colouring, yes. But I don't have her tolerance for the weakness of human nature. Or her belief in the ultimate good to be found in others,' Rogan added. 'My father was a prime example of that particular myth!'

The frown deepened between Elizabeth's eyes. 'I found him an easy man to work for and get along with during the week I knew him…'

'Next you'll be telling me he spoke lovingly of his wife and son!' Rogan said in disbelief. 'When in reality it must have been difficult to know Brad had even *had* a wife, let alone a son, when there isn't a single family photograph in the house.'

Elizabeth wasn't a woman for a lot of clutter herself, but even she had several photographs of her mother on show in her apartment in London. Something that was definitely noticeably lacking at Sullivan House…

'My father had all the photographs removed and put away after my mother died,' Rogan explained grimly, a nerve pulsing in his tightly clenched jaw.

Elizabeth's face softened in sympathy. 'Perhaps it was just too painful for him to see reminders of your mother around the house every day?'

'Oh, yes, I'm sure that must have been very painful,' Rogan bit out. 'I'm not sure I would want a daily visual reminder of someone I'd killed, either!'

Someone he'd *killed*?

Was Rogan really saying that Brad Sullivan had killed his wife?

## CHAPTER FOUR

'YOU can't possibly believe that?' Elizabeth gasped incredulously, when she could finally speak at all, her cheeks pale and her eyes wide as she stared across the width of the table at Rogan.

Not surprising, really, Rogan accepted grimly. It couldn't be every day she heard a man accuse his own father of being responsible for killing his mother!

He stood up abruptly. 'Let's get out of here,' he rasped.

Elizabeth Brown continued to stare at him as she rose unsteadily to her feet, belatedly turning back to pick up her shoulder bag at she realised she had forgotten it in her obvious shock at his statement.

'Rogan?' she prompted shakily once they were outside on the pavement.

Rogan's fingers curled about the top of her arm, his face stern as he walked across the square to where Elizabeth had parked the car. 'Brad wasn't standing behind my mother pushing her when she fell off the cliff to her death,' he explained. 'But the adulterous snake might just as well have been!' he added coldly.

Elizabeth's head was buzzing with the things Rogan had

just said about his parents. But not so much that she wasn't completely aware of the touch of those lean fingers wrapped strongly about her upper arm… 'I—I don't know what to say…'

Rogan's mouth twisted derisively as he watched her fumbling in her shoulder bag for her car keys. 'That must make you unique amongst your sex!'

Elizabeth was aware that Rogan was probably being flippant as a means of alleviating the intensity of their conversation, but that didn't make his deliberate taunt any less insulting. 'You really are a male chauvinist, aren't you?' she muttered as she finally found her keys and unlocked the doors.

Rogan quirked an eyebrow. 'If I was a male chauvinist I wouldn't allow you to do the driving.'

Elizabeth frowned at him over the top of her bottle-green Mini. 'It's *my* car!'

He gave an unconcerned shrug. 'I believe chauvinists are only concerned with their own fragile egos rather than ownership.' He opened the passenger door and climbed inside.

Leaving Elizabeth with no choice but to do the same. All the time aware that there was nothing in the least fragile about this man's ego!

She gave Rogan another frowning glance before switching on the ignition and driving out of the town square and on to the coast road that led back to Sullivan House.

The coast road consisted mainly of high cliffs that dropped down to the beach or the rocks below. The same high cliffs from which Rogan's mother had fallen to her death…?

For some reason Elizabeth had thought that Maggie Sullivan's premature death had been from some unnamed illness. To learn that she had actually fallen to her death from these high cliffs because her husband had been an 'adulterous snake' was more than disturbing in view of the behaviour of Elizabeth's own father, and her mother's response to it…

As a result of that, Elizabeth had deliberately kept her own adult life free of emotional entanglements; she certainly didn't welcome anything that reminded her of the pain and disillusionment that had been so much a part of her own childhood.

Perhaps it might be better if she postponed cataloguing the library at Sullivan House for now and came back later in the summer, when things might be less emotionally fraught?

When Rogan had returned to New York and was no longer present at Sullivan House to disturb her, for instance…

And she was once again disturbed—by his close proximity in the confines of her car!

Barely leashed power oozed from every pore of Rogan's muscular body, sending out a purely physical challenge that heightened Elizabeth's senses, both sight and smell. Her fingers tightened about the steering wheel as she resisted the urge to reach out and touch the lean strength of his hands where they lay clenched on his powerful thighs.

She'd never reacted to a man in this way. At least…she never had until Rogan Sullivan's sudden appearance at Sullivan House last night. Since then her nerve-endings—and every other part of her!—had been on constant alert.

'What are you thinking about?' he suddenly wanted to know.

Elizabeth's fingers gripped the steering wheel even tighter. 'I was simply wondering if your long hair is a reaction to being in the army for so many years, or if you've just forgotten to go to a barber recently.'

'Liar,' Rogan murmured huskily, well aware that Elizabeth had been shooting him surreptitious glances from beneath those sooty lashes for the last few minutes. And he was experienced enough to know that Elizabeth Brown was aroused by what she saw when she looked at him.

Her eyes were fever-bright. Her cheeks were flushed. Her breathing was soft and uneven. Also, her breasts were full, with the nipples showing hard and aroused against the soft material of her blouse.

Every starchy inch of Elizabeth Brown was aware of him, and he found that knowledge delicious!

She bristled at the accusation. 'I—'

'You're clenching your left hand again, Elizabeth,' he warned softly.

She frowned at the observation, but instantly lessened the tightness of the grip she had on the steering wheel. 'You—'

'Admit it, Liza.' He deliberately gave her that sexy smile as he used the name he knew she objected to so strongly. 'When you look at me, you like what you see!'

Her jaw tightened disapprovingly, although the blush in her cheeks and the catching of her breath in her throat told a completely different story… 'I told you not to call me—'

'I like calling you Liza.' Rogan turned in his seat so that he could look at her fully. 'With your eyes shining brightly, and that colour in your cheeks, you're much more of a Liza than you are a stiff and unapproachable Elizabeth,' he said appreciatively.

'Stiff and—!' She gave an impatient shake of her head. 'Are you deliberately trying to annoy me?'

He quirked dark brows. 'Am I succeeding?'

'Very much so!'

He grinned unrepentantly. 'Enough to make sure that you definitely decide to high-tail it out of Sullivan House as soon as you can make the appropriate excuses?'

That blush in her cheeks deepened as she gasped softly. 'How did you know…?'

'That's what you were thinking about doing a few minutes ago,' Rogan finished dryly. 'You're pretty easy to read, Elizabeth.' He gave an unconcerned shrug. Rogan hadn't just learned to analyse computers over the last fifteen years; he had learned to read people too.

Although this woman was a little more complicated than most. No, make that a *lot* more complicated!

Why did a beautiful woman in her late twenties bury herself in academia? To such an extent that she even chose to occupy her vacation time buried in the wilds of Cornwall, cataloguing a private library? Did she ever let anyone past that spiky exterior? Rogan wondered. More to the point, had she ever let a man past that bristly exterior and into her body…?

Elizabeth wasn't sure she liked Rogan finding her 'easy to read'—especially considering some of the thoughts she had been having about him since first setting eyes on him the previous night!

Her mouth firmed. 'I have no intention of "high-tailing it out of Sullivan House", as you put it.' Not any more, she didn't. Not when he seemed to have so easily guessed that *he* would be the reason for her leaving! 'Your father engaged me to catalogue his library, and if you still want me to continue, then I will fulfil that obligation.'

His mouth twisted. 'Big on obligation, are you?'

Elizabeth stiffened at the taunt she heard in his tone. 'I

believe that once given a person's word should be honoured, yes.'

Implying, Rogan would guess, that someone close to her—or someone she had allowed close to her?—had once let her down pretty badly.

He nodded. 'Are you hoping to find even more valuable first editions?'

'It's possible, yes,' she acknowledged cautiously.

Rogan chuckled softly. 'You don't have to be so cagey, Elizabeth, I'm not about to steal any of them and sell them off for a huge profit!'

'It would hardly be stealing when the books appear to be yours now,' she reasoned.

'But you do think I'm going to sell them off for profit at the first opportunity, don't you? Don't bother to deny it, Elizabeth.' His tone was grim now, as he saw the truth of his accusation in her face. 'You're obviously as big on making assumptions about people as you are on honouring your obligations!' he accused, with obvious disgust.

Was she? Elizabeth wondered. Perhaps. Where this particular man was concerned, anyway. He seriously threatened her peace of mind…

'I— What are you doing in here?' Elizabeth came to a stop in the library doorway as she saw Rogan, sitting behind his father's leather-topped mahogany desk, her laptop open in front of him.

He looked up to raise an unimpressed eyebrow. 'As the new owner, don't you think I have a perfect right to be in here?'

Well…of course he had a right to enter his father's library. *His* library now. Elizabeth was just surprised, having come to the library with the intention of working again this afternoon, once she had been upstairs to freshen up after they'd returned from town, to find Rogan had beaten her to it.

She stood in front of the desk to arch her own auburn brows. 'Find anything of interest on my laptop?'

Rogan sat back. '*Your* laptop?' he murmured slowly. 'I thought it was my father's.'

Elizabeth smiled at having at last been able to disconcert a man who was so self-confident he made her want to scream. 'I prefer to work with equipment I'm familiar with.'

There it was again, Rogan noted with a frown. Elizabeth Brown liked her life ordered and predictable, even down to the laptop she used for whatever work she happened to be doing.

Rogan grimaced. 'I had some e-mails I wanted to send.' Damn it, if he had known this was Elizabeth's laptop he might have had a look through some of her other files. Just in the interest of gaining further insight into what made her tick, of course. It was something Rogan was always careful to do with the people that were around him on a day-to-day basis.

He already knew what Elizabeth did; it was the rest of the information on her that was still a little sketchy. Where she came from. Who her family was. Who her friends were.

For different reasons, most probably, Elizabeth kept her personal life as close to her chest as Rogan did his own…

'Sorry about that.' He shut the laptop down before standing up, his eyes narrowing at the instinctive way Elizabeth instantly took a step away from him.

What the hell?

Was this woman *scared* of him?

No, that wasn't fear Rogan could see in her eyes, but something else. Something much more interesting…

Elizabeth took another step back as Rogan moved out from behind the desk, once again finding herself overwhelmed by the sheer animal magnetism of the man. He really was like that predator she had been reading about last night, his movements slow and stealthy, soundless on the carpeted floor. The muscles moved smoothly in his legs and beneath his tight-fitting T-shirt as he came ever closer, the very air about him seeming to part in deference to all that rippling power.

Her eyes were wide with apprehension. 'I— What are you doing?'

He raised dark brows over those inky eyes. 'What does it look like I'm doing?' Even his voice sounded lower, husky, purposeful…

Elizabeth swallowed hard. 'I came in here to work—'

'Later.'

'Later?' she repeated, with a nervous sweep of her tongue across suddenly dry lips.

The blackness of Rogan's gaze locked on to that nervous movement. 'Later,' he confirmed gruffly.

He was standing so close to her now that Elizabeth could feel the heat of his body enveloping her, and that heat and the subtle scent of him were acting like a drug on her already heightened senses.

The same senses that had been on alert from the moment she first set eyes on this man.

Sight. Smell. Touch…

Elizabeth gave a shake of her head in an effort to clear her mind of the foggy haze that seemed to be encompassing her. 'I don't know what game you're playing, Rogan—'

'I never play games, Liza,' he assured her softly.

He had called her by that hateful name again, but for the moment Elizabeth was too concerned by the threat he represented to her, to her equilibrium, to bother correcting him. 'You're playing one right now. And it isn't funny,' she reproved.

Rogan didn't find this situation funny, either. In fact, he deeply regretted having started this, and was no longer sure who was challenging whom.

Elizabeth's eyes were such a deep and drowning blue. Those sooty lashes a dark sweep against the creaminess of her cheeks. Her mouth, those full and pouting lips that had just felt the moist touch of her tongue, was tempting him to do the same. She smelled so damned good too: a mixture of some elusive floral scent and a warm and sexy femininity…

Rogan gave a low groan in his throat as he felt his body respond to her, his thighs stirring, hardening, pulsing.

Aching!

'Rogan…?'

Even the way she spoke his name, so huskily, so warily, was arousing. Too much so for Rogan to be able to resist tasting her. Just one taste, he promised himself. One taste of her lips, with the feel of those slender curves pressed against his much harder ones, the crush of the softness of her breasts against his chest, her thighs against his, and he would let her go.

Elizabeth barely had time to raise her hands, with the intention of warding Rogan off, before his arms moved about her. He pulled her in tightly against the hardness of his body and his head lowered so that his mouth could claim hers.

Fiercely. Hungrily. Crushing, parting her lips beneath his as he deepened the kiss. His tongue surged past her lips and into the heated cavern of her mouth.

The hands she had raised to hold Rogan at bay instead

clung to him. Her fingers curled into the front of his T-shirt as she met and returned the intensity of that kiss. Those fingers tightened and she held on to the black material for support as desire ripped shockingly through her body. She could feel her breasts swelling, the nipples hard and aching, the warmth between her thighs becoming a burning sensation as she felt herself becoming wet and swollen with a need she had never known before.

She could feel the pulse of Rogan's arousal against the flatness of her stomach as he pressed her even closer against him. Every long, thick, hard inch of him throbbed rhythmically against her, in a promise that would ease the increasing ache between Elizabeth's own thighs as he surged powerfully inside her.

Rogan knew he had to stop this. Now. Before things got completely out of control.

Except she tasted so good. Felt so good. The softness of her curves was a perfect fit against the hardness of his.

All of her was perfect, Rogan discovered as he moved his hand beneath her blouse to touch the silky heat of her bare flesh, caressing upwards, until his fingers curved about the soft, up-tilting swell of her breast. Not too small. Not too large. Just a perfect fit in the palm of his hand.

His own body throbbed anew as Elizabeth gave a throaty groan and her head dropped back to break the kiss. As Rogan moved the soft pad of his thumb against the puckered pout of her nipple her breathing becoming laboured and ragged, and he kissed down the length of her creamy throat to push aside the collar of her blouse so that his tongue and teeth could seek out the hollows at the base of her neck.

She tasted better than anything Rogan had ever experienced before. The feel of her skin against his lips was a beguiling combination of feminine softness and spice.

He could feel the heat of Elizabeth's arousal as she pressed her hips into his, sensed how ready she was for him.

So ready Rogan wanted to lie her down on the carpeted floor and take her right here and now. To thrust into her time and time again, until she screamed out his name as she climaxed, wildly, fiercely, as spasm after spasm of pleasure wrapped itself around him and she took him over that edge with her.

Rogan nudged her back towards the desk, feeling the added pressure of her body against his as the wood pressed against the back of her legs. He pushed those legs apart to step in between them, grinding his arousal against her tempting heat in an effort to relieve some of the fierceness of his own need.

He succeeded only in increasing that need until he could only move rhythmically against her, the barrier of their clothing no hindrance to the heat, the satisfaction he found between Elizabeth's legs as he continued to surge against her. Again and again. Harder. Faster. Until Rogan felt he would lose his mind if he didn't soon possess her for real!

This was insane, Elizabeth acknowledged achingly, as she felt the thick length of Rogan's shaft pressed against the swollen nub between her legs, creating a fire deep inside her that quickly spread and threatened to flame totally out of control.

She couldn't do this…

She *wouldn't* do this!

'No, Rogan!' she gasped, even as she pushed against the hardness of his chest. 'No!' she cried again, entangling her fingers in his over-long dark hair and pulling his head back and away from her when her verbal protest had no effect on those questing, arousing lips. 'No,' she said again firmly, and she looked up appealingly into the unfocused darkness of his eyes.

Eyes as wild, dark, and dangerous as those of the lethal predator she had initially thought him to be!

The very air between them seemed to crackle with tension, and Elizabeth could only wait tensely to see if her pleas would have any effect. Because if they didn't then she knew she was seriously in danger, crushed as she was between Rogan and the desk, every hard muscle and sinew of his body imprinted upon her own. There was no way, absolutely no way, that she would be able to physically fight off a man as large and fit as Rogan undoubtedly was. And at this moment, breathing in his scent, still weak from the touch of his hands against the bareness of her flesh, she wasn't sure that she really wanted to…

She continued to stare up at him for long, timeless seconds, not breathing, not moving, the palms of her hands damp with tension, her legs trembling beneath her.

His jaw clenched even as the fierceness slowly left the dark unfathomable depths of his eyes. He stepped abruptly away from her, the muscles still tense in his back as he turned away from her to smooth the wildness of his hair back from his face and draw deep, controlling breaths into his lungs.

Allowing Elizabeth to draw in a couple of much-needed breaths herself.

What on earth had happened just now? More to the point, how had it happened?

She rarely even dated, let alone allowed men to get close to her in this way. This totally physical way!

She hadn't exactly *allowed* Rogan to get close to her; he had just taken the opportunity.

And she had responded…

Responded to that animal magnetism that drew her like a moth to a flame. To the hunger of his lips on hers. To the caress of his hand against the bareness of her skin. To the fierceness of his hard and demanding thighs pressed so intimately against hers…

Elizabeth felt another warm rush of heat between her legs just at remembering the hardness of Rogan's thighs pressed against the throb of her own arousal. An arousal he had found with unerring accuracy as he rubbed himself against her and took her ever higher, ever nearer to a release she had never known.

She had wanted Rogan just now. Desperately. So much so that she wouldn't have been able to stop him if he had chosen to continue kissing and touching her. If he had thrown off their clothes before laying her back on the desk and satisfying their desire for one another.

Dear God…!

# CHAPTER FIVE

ROGAN was still breathing raggedly as he turned back to face Elizabeth. 'Well, that was—'

'Stupid!' she supplied forcefully, her cheeks flushed and her eyes brightly accusing, her breasts rapidly rising and falling beneath her blouse in her agitation.

His mouth compressed. 'I was going to say *unexpected…*'

This spiky woman—a lecturer in History who catalogued libraries in her spare time, for heaven's sake!—simply wasn't his type. Absolutely not.

Except it had aroused Rogan just to be able to pierce through all that prim self-righteousness. To see this obviously controlled woman totally come apart in his arms…

Rogan lived his life as he wanted. As he chose. And where he chose. With no involvements, emotional or otherwise. That had worked for him for the past fifteen years, and he fully intended for it to continue working for him for the foreseeable future.

Even if Elizabeth Brown had succeeded in getting to him, in breaching his guard, in a way Rogan couldn't remember any other woman ever doing before…

His mouth thinned. 'You're right, it was stupid,' he acknowledged harshly. 'Let's just forg— ' He broke off as his mobile began to vibrate against his hip. 'Excuse me.' He took the mobile off his belt to take the call—no doubt a telephoned answer to one of the e-mails he had just sent.

Elizabeth didn't know which of them she was most angry with. Herself for having responded to Rogan in the way she had. Or Rogan for the way he had so readily agreed their behaviour had been stupid.

The latter, probably…

'Tell her I'll call her when I have the time,' Rogan said decisively into his mobile, even as he kept his coldly dark gaze fixed steadily on Elizabeth. 'I don't give a damn what she wants, Grant; you can tell her I'll call her when I'm good and ready!'

*Her? Don't give a damn what she wants? I'll her call when I'm good and ready…*

Rogan couldn't have told Elizabeth any more clearly that there was already a woman in his life. No doubt a woman who also lived in New York. A woman who had believed she could trust Rogan to be apart from her for the few days he would be in England without the fear that he would end up with another woman in his arms.

Another woman who had allowed Rogan to kiss and touch her in a way she had never been kissed and touched before!

'What did I do wrong now?'

Elizabeth had been so full of self-condemnation for her own gullibility that she hadn't even realised Rogan had ended his call and was now studying her from between narrowed lids. 'Who said you had done anything wrong?' She glared at him.

He scowled. 'Your disgusted expression said it for you.'

Elizabeth scowled at him. 'I can't imagine what makes you think that.'

'Male intuition?'

'Men don't have intuition!' she flashed back.

'Ah.' He grimaced. 'You're one of *those*.'

Her eyes widened. 'I *beg* your pardon?'

Rogan shrugged. 'A man-hater.'

Elizabeth felt heat in her cheeks at the taunt. 'I *don't* hate men.'

'Just me, hmm?' he said knowingly.

Elizabeth only wished that she *did* hate this man. But the truth was just being in the same room with Rogan disturbed her more than any other man ever had. As for being kissed by him, touched by him…!

'Not at all, Rogan,' she denied coolly. 'But I had no sooner walked in here and found you using my laptop than you began kissing me—which begs the question, how did you get past my personal security code?' Elizabeth frowned as she suddenly realised access to her computer was supposed to be protected by that code. *Supposed* to be. It obviously hadn't been enough to stop Rogan from accessing it.

So much for Rogan's thinking that kissing Elizabeth might divert her attention away from the fact that he had been using her laptop earlier!

'You really don't want to know.'

Her stance became one of stubborn determination. 'Oh, I really think I do.'

Rogan smiled nastily. 'I have a doctorate in Computer Analysis, remember.'

Auburn brows rose challengingly. 'And that allows you

to violate another person's personal laptop any time you feel like it?'

It actually allowed Rogan to access almost any computer system anywhere in the world any time he felt like it!

He grimaced. 'More or less.'

Elizabeth folded her arms in front of her chest. 'How much more or less?'

Elizabeth Brown was dogged as well as intelligent, Rogan acknowledged ruefully. 'Give me a computer, almost any computer, and I guarantee that in a matter of minutes I will have access to all its stored information.' He gave an unapologetic smile.

'Isn't that illegal?'

Rogan's smile widened into a hard grin. 'Some might call it that, yes.'

Her mouth thinned. 'What do *you* call it?'

'Useful.'

Elizabeth gave a disgusted shake of her head at the complete lack of apology in his tone. 'And you don't see anything wrong in that?'

Rogan made an impatient movement. 'Why should I, if it gets the job done?'

She became very still. 'What sort of job could you possibly do that requires that you intrude on information stored on other people's computers?'

He snorted. 'If I told you that I might have to kill you afterwards!'

'Stop teasing me, Rogan.'

'Who says I'm teasing?' He quirked dark brows.

'*I* do.' Elizabeth glared at him.

'I'm not in the habit of explaining myself or my actions

to anyone, Elizabeth. And, where I come from, sharing a few kisses with someone doesn't give them the right to question, or to poke and prod into other parts of that person's life.'

She drew her breath in sharply. 'I wasn't—'

'Oh, yes, you most certainly were,' he rasped. 'And, enjoyable as those kisses were—and probably would be again, given the opportunity—'

'Which there *won't* be!'

'I think you should know that I don't do permanent relationships!' Rogan concluded harshly, as if she hadn't interrupted.

Elizabeth had never felt so uncomfortable and humiliated in the whole of her life!

Rogan couldn't have told her any more clearly not to read anything into the kisses they had just shared. As if! Elizabeth was as anxious to forget them as he obviously was.

She gave him a scathing glance. 'Well, that's just fine—because neither do I!'

He looked at her speculatively. 'Does that mean you do casual instead?'

'It means that where you're concerned I don't do any sort of relationship whatsoever! We're only here together at all because of circumstances.' And Elizabeth wished now that she hadn't been goaded into staying on. 'I suggest that for the rest of your time here we stay well out of each other's way!'

Rogan gave a terse inclination of his head. 'I'm glad we got that straightened out.'

'So am I!' Elizabeth had never felt quite so much like hitting someone as she did Rogan at that moment.

He gave a slow, taunting smile. 'Does that mean you won't be joining me for dinner?'

Dinner? Elizabeth was so angry—with herself as much

as Rogan—that she wasn't sure she would be able to eat anything for the rest of the day!

Her chin rose. 'I'll be quite happy to have a tray in my room.'

'That seems a little unfriendly, don't you think?'

A frown appeared between her eyes. 'I thought we had just agreed that neither of us *does* friendly?'

'Oh, I do friendly. Just not for ever.' Rogan regarded her mockingly. 'Did you eat dinner on a tray in your room when my father was here?'

'No, of course not.'

'Then you don't need to do it now, either,' he pointed out.

Need? What Elizabeth *needed* was some time—and space—away from Rogan Sullivan, in which to regain some of her shattered composure. 'I would like to get on with some work now, if you don't mind.' She deliberately turned her back on him.

'No problem,' Rogan came back nonchalantly. 'I'll see you at dinner.'

Elizabeth continued to stand unmoving in the middle of the library long after she knew Rogan had gone.

Rogan had kissed her, and she had kissed him back. Damn it, she hadn't just kissed him, she had been hungry for him! Hadn't been able to get enough of him! To get close enough to him! Still ached with wanting him…

He was everything she had ever fantasised about. Everything she had never thought to encounter in her quite frankly boring academic life, she told herself wryly.

Maybe.

But for her to have totally lost all inhibition with a man she knew nothing about was seriously worrying.

She knew Rogan had kissed her as if he'd wanted to

devour her. As if he'd wanted to taste and touch every part of her. As if he'd wanted to bury himself deep inside her and—

She knew *nothing* positive about the man!

Rogan had arrived in the middle of the night. The only way of contacting him was through a PO Box in New York. He had used her laptop, somehow bypassing the security code, without even bothering to check who it belonged to. He had totally dismissed the need to contact his girlfriend.

Worst of all, he was mysterious about his past, and obviously had no intention of sharing any important details about himself with her.

Elizabeth hadn't just been stupid when she had responded so wantonly to Rogan, she had behaved totally recklessly. And reckless was something that she never was where a man was concerned. Let alone a man who had so reminded her of her father, with his claim of wanting no permanent ties in his life…

Leonard Brown. Handsome. Charming. Secretive. And totally immoral…

Leonard had been working for industrialist James Britten as one of the man's senior managers when he had first seen Stella Britten. A tiny red-haired beauty of only twenty-one. Adored by her father, and surrounded by dozens of young men who wished to capture her heart, Stella had barely noticed thirty-year-old Leonard on the occasions when she visited her father at his office..

Then Stella's father had died unexpectedly, and suddenly Leonard was there, offering comfort, a shoulder to cry on, someone to lean on. Offering to help her deal with everything that needed to be dealt with now that her father was dead. James Britten had left no son to inherit. Only Stella, his beautiful, oh-so-grateful and very quickly so-much-in-love-with-Leonard and pregnant daughter.

The two had been married within six months of James Britten's dying, and, although the company had had to remain in Stella's possession, Leonard had taken over as chairman within three months of their marriage. Something that had suited Leonard perfectly, as he had been able to leave the work to others whilst he wined and dined and travelled abroad 'on business'.

Over the years Leonard had found a woman, or women, in every foreign city he visited—despite the fact that he'd had a wife and daughter waiting for him at home in London.

A wife who had loved him so much she had been willing to overlook Leonard's affairs as long as he always came home to her. But as the years had slowly passed she had become more and more disenchanted and bitter over the man who simply couldn't, or wouldn't, remain faithful to her. To the extent that Stella had eventually begun drinking whenever Leonard was away from home, in an effort to block out all thought of him with those other women.

Stella had been drinking heavily the night she had driven into a brick wall and been killed instantly…

Eighteen-year-old Elizabeth had stood beside her mother's newly covered grave only days later, and had watched as her father wept for his dead and disillusioned wife. She had sworn to herself there and then that she would never, *ever* love someone in the same helpless way that her mother had loved her father.

In the same way Maggie Sullivan had loved *her* husband?

It was ironic—unbelievable, really—that two people who were as unalike as Elizabeth and Rogan undoubtedly were had both been shaped into the adults they now were by the unhappiness of their parents' marriages.

Elizabeth: solitary, serious and academic, determined never to fall in love.

Rogan: just as solitary, but wild and untamed—untameable!—and just as determined never to fall in love…

'Glass of red wine?' Rogan indicated the glass he held. 'Elizabeth?' he prompted with a frown as she made no effort to move away from the doorway of the drawing room.

But for the moment Elizabeth couldn't move. In fact, she had been rooted to the spot from the moment she had first entered the room and seen Rogan.

A Rogan who looked so handsome this evening he literally took her breath away!

Over the last twenty-four hours she had become accustomed to seeing him in the black clothing and boots he habitually wore, and which somehow seemed to suit the aura of danger that always surrounded him.

Tonight he wore a silk shirt the colour of freshly brewed espresso coffee that hinted at the muscled chest beneath rather than emphasised it, and a pair of expertly tailored trousers in the same dark coffee colour. With his long hair brushed back from that intelligent brow, and those dark, enigmatic eyes, Rogan appeared every bit as threatening, if not more so, as he had in the black clothing he preferred.

'Elizabeth?' Rogan pressed again impatiently; what on earth was wrong with the woman?

After her earlier comments concerning the clothes he wore, he had decided to change before dinner. But as the time to eat had drawn nearer, with no sign of Elizabeth, he had been starting to wonder if she was going to join him after all. If he hadn't frightened her off completely earlier this afternoon after almost taking her on top of his father's desk!

Only to turn a few seconds ago and see her standing in the doorway. Unmoving, and warily silent. So far in their acquaintance Elizabeth had seemed to have plenty to say about everything. Including himself.

Not that it was any chore to just look at her. Her auburn hair was arranged in its usual perky style, those sooty lashes perfectly framed the deep blue of her eyes, and she had brushed a peach gloss onto the fullness of her lips. In a fitted knee-length sleeveless dress of midnight-blue silk, Elizabeth was certainly easy on the eye.

Who would ever have guessed that, beneath those unflattering cotton pyjamas and the tailored trousers she had worn today, Elizabeth Brown had the most gloriously sexy legs Rogan had ever seen? Lightly tanned, they were slender and shapely, the ankles appearing delicate above the two-inch heels of the strappy dark blue sandals she wore.

Dr Elizabeth Brown wasn't just beautiful; she was hot!

'No red wine for me, thank you.' The snappy anger in the deep blue of her eyes as she walked further into the room told Rogan that she had noted his admiring gaze and didn't appreciate it.

Well, that was just too bad. If she didn't want anyone to look—didn't want Rogan to look—then she should have stayed in the safe businesslike black trousers and blouse!

Rogan looked amused. 'Is that because you would prefer white wine, or would you like something else instead?'

'No, thank you. I don't drink alcohol,' Elizabeth answered abruptly as she sat down in one of the armchairs. 'At all,' she added, just so that there should be no more confusion.

'Good for you,' he drawled, before moving to sit in the armchair opposite hers, that dark gaze narrow and enigmatic. 'Do you smoke?'

'No.'

'Take drugs?'

Her mouth thinned in distaste. 'Certainly not!'

'Sleep with married men?'

Her gaze narrowed impatiently. 'Rogan—'

'Just kidding!' He grinned, even as he held up his hand in apology. 'So, you're a woman without vices…'

It was a statement rather than a question, and Elizabeth didn't bother to answer. How could she when this afternoon she had literally melted in this man's arms?

'How about you, Rogan? Obviously you drink alcohol.'

'In moderation,' he put in softly, and he raised his glass in a silent toast to her before taking a sip of the ruby-red wine.

'Smoke?'

'Not for years.'

'Take drugs?'

'Never,' he answered, as flatly as she had earlier.

Elizabeth raised auburn brows. 'Sleep with married women?'

'Again, never,' he stated.

Her mouth twisted humourlessly. 'How about *unmarried* women?'

'I'm thirty-three years old, Elizabeth; what do you think?' he taunted with a hard grin.

Elizabeth thought she should never have joined in this ridiculous conversation! 'I think, as you pointed out earlier—' oh-so-succinctly! '—that it's none of my business!'

Rogan's grin widened, his teeth very white and even against that bronzed skin. 'My guess is you didn't mean to ask that last question.'

No, she hadn't. Of *course* Rogan Sullivan slept with unmarried women—although 'slept with' was probably a complete misnomer for what *he* did when he was in bed with a woman!

Elizabeth wasn't happy about the way his dark gaze followed the movement as she nervously crossed one bare knee over the other…

She instantly uncrossed them. 'Perhaps we should go through to dinner?'

'You seem a little…tense this evening, Elizabeth?' He met her gaze with steady intensity.

Her eyes widened. 'I'm not in the least tense.'

'No?'

'No!' Elizabeth denied vehemently, knowing that her tone, and the way she stood up so suddenly, instantly gave the lie to her claim.

What was it about this man that made her so uncomfortable? So on edge? So totally removed from her normally composed and efficient self? Whatever it was, she had better put a stop to it.

'I believe it's time we went in to dinner,' she reminded him again, more evenly this time.

'Fine,' he agreed lightly, and he rose smoothly to his feet beside her.

Instantly making Elizabeth's already raw and sensitive nerve-endings thrum!

She didn't drink alcohol, or smoke, or sleep with men—married or otherwise—but just being in the same room with Rogan made her dearly wish she did the latter, at least. Every time she was anywhere near this man she felt the urge to rip the clothes from his body and have her way with him. Her very *wicked* way with him!

Rogan watched the emotions flicker across Elizabeth's flushed and expressive face as she looked at him: tension, then desire, quickly followed by dismay. 'I'd give a thousand dollars to know what your thoughts were just now,' he murmured throatily.

Her eyes widened in alarm before she quickly looked away. 'You would be wasting your money.'

'It's my money to waste.'

She shrugged. 'I was only thinking of the books I intend cataloguing tomorrow.'

Rogan gave a casual glance down at Elizabeth's left hand, knowing by the way it was clenched that she wasn't telling the truth. Knowing by the way she instantly unclenched her hand that she knew he knew it too!

'Having a giveaway is annoying, isn't it?' he murmured conversationally.

Her chin rose determinedly. 'I have no idea what you mean.'

'Sure you don't…' he drawled.

'I believe you now owe me a thousand dollars…'

He gave a rueful shake of his head. 'We both know you just lied and I don't owe you a damn thing.' Rogan stood back to allow her to precede him out of the room, his politeness owing as much to the fact that he wanted to continue admiring her legs and the gentle sway of her hips as she walked in front of him to the dining room as it did to good manners.

They certainly hadn't had lecturers like Elizabeth Brown when he'd worked on getting his degree!

'When did you say you intended returning to the States?' Elizabeth asked Rogan coolly, once Mrs Baines had left the room after serving the first course of smoked salmon.

The two of them were once again seated at the small family dining table. The evening sun shining in through the huge bay window made the lighting of the candles on the table unnecessary. Thank goodness! Candlelight would have made it appear too much like a romantic dinner for two…

Something this most certainly wasn't!

Elizabeth didn't fool herself for a moment, and knew that ordinarily Rogan wouldn't have even noticed a woman like her. She felt sure that his usual taste in women ran to something a little more exotic than a university lecturer who, at the age of twenty-eight, neither drank, smoked, nor slept around.

In fact, the phrase 'beggars can't be choosers' came to mind!

Rogan scowled darkly. 'I don't remember saying when I was leaving.'

She frowned slightly. 'I had assumed that you would only be staying until after your father's funeral?'

'Never heard the one about assumption being the mother of all cock-ups?' he asked.

She gave an inclination of her head. 'As necessity is the mother of invention?'

'Something like that.' Rogan grimaced. 'I suppose I'll have to stay until after my father's funeral,' he accepted tightly.

'I would have thought so, yes.' Elizabeth frowned at his obvious reluctance.

'I'm many things, Elizabeth, but I've never thought a hypocrite was one of them.' His mouth twisted with distaste.

'Even so…'

'Even so…' he conceded dryly. 'No doubt you're a dutiful daughter and visit your own parents once a week? Probably for Sunday lunch?'

Elizabeth didn't know what to say in answer to that. What could she say when she hadn't so much as seen her own father since the argument that had followed the reading of her mother's will ten years ago?

'No doubt,' she answered stiltedly.

Rogan's gaze became piercing as he heard the lack of conviction in Elizabeth's tone. 'Or perhaps dinner on a Friday evening?'

'Perhaps.'

Rogan was certain of the hollowness to her tone that time… 'Or perhaps, like me, you prefer to stay the hell away from them?'

Warm colour crept up into the pallor of her cheeks. 'I don't believe this conversation was about me—'

'Sure it was.' Rogan gave up all pretence of eating the smoked salmon and sat back in his chair to study her through narrowed lids. 'We can do this the hard way or the easy way, Elizabeth. Your choice.'

'I don't think—'

'Okay, the hard way.' He shrugged. 'Are both your parents still alive?'

Her jaw hardened. 'No.'

'Both dead?'

'No.'

'Mother dead?'

'Yes.'

'Father?'

A nerve pulsed in that clenched jaw. 'Rogan—'

'Don't like to talk about yourself much, do you?' he jeered. 'Just humour me, hmm, Elizabeth,' he murmured.

She gave a deep sigh. 'My father is still very much alive.'

'And?'

She scowled. 'And nothing.'

Rogan gave a slow, taunting smile. 'Admit it, Elizabeth—you don't like the louse any more than I liked my own father!'

She winced. 'It isn't a question of liking or disliking. My father and I lead completely different lives. He—he remarried not long after my mother died, ten years ago.'

And that must have hurt, Rogan guessed easily. 'Wicked stepmother?'

'I wouldn't know; I've never met her,' Elizabeth answered coolly.

'How about your father? Do you still see him?'

'We exchange Christmas cards. And he has my mobile number in case of emergencies,' Elizabeth admitted tightly.

'And?'

Her mouth twisted humourlessly. 'So far there haven't been any.'

Rogan sensed the same anger that he felt towards his own father burning deep down inside her. 'It would seem that we have more in common than we originally thought, Elizabeth…' he muttered.

On the surface Rogan knew that he and Elizabeth were nothing alike. But nevertheless he would guess that the two of them had both been shaped by their childhoods: the premature death of an adored mother, and a fractured love/hate relationship with the father that remained.

Deep down, where it really mattered, he and Elizabeth were more alike than Rogan liked.

Or wanted them to be…

# CHAPTER SIX

'WHERE are you off to so early in the morning?'

Elizabeth had almost reached the bottom of the stairs, the rucksack containing her costume and towel draped over one shoulder, when she heard Rogan's voice behind her and turned to see him standing on the wide gallery above, looking down at her.

As he said, it was still early in the morning—only a little after seven o'clock—but, like her, Rogan was already up and dressed, his T-shirt once again black, as were his jeans, the dark length of his hair slightly damp, probably from the shower.

As usual, Elizabeth was instantly, nerve-janglingly aware of him…

She maintained her cool expression with effort. 'I like to go for a swim first thing in the morning.'

She felt even more in need of a wake-up swim today, after the conversation about her father at dinner the previous evening had brought back all those unhappy memories and caused her to have an almost sleepless night.

Rogan scowled darkly. 'Where?'

'At my health club when I'm in London, but here I make do with the sea.' The sea water wasn't doing much for her complexion or her hair, but Elizabeth had always enjoyed swimming as a way of kick-starting her day, and saw no reason to change that routine when she could so easily walk down to the sandy cove below the cliffs.

Rogan looked at her speculatively. 'And my guess is you've been doing that every morning since you came here,' he said.

Elizabeth's brows rose. 'Of course.'

'Alone?'

'Yes…'

'Without informing anyone where you were going?' His voice had become dangerously soft.

'Rogan—'

'Hell's bells, woman, are you stupid or do you just have a death wish?' Rogan rasped impatiently as he descended the stairs two at a time until he was standing beside her, glaring down at her.

Elizabeth had to tilt her head back slightly in order to meet that glittering gaze head-on. 'As far as I'm aware I'm neither of those things. I simply like to swim first thing in the morning—'

'In a sea where the current is precarious at best and downright dangerous at worst!' Angry heat emanated from Rogan's body, and his hands were clenched at his sides.

Elizabeth frowned. 'I assure you, I'm always very careful.'

'This is Cornwall, Elizabeth,' he snapped. 'The worst place on the south coast for shipwrecks and drowning. There's no such thing as being very careful!'

'Rogan—'

'Don't even *attempt* to use that patronising tone on me,' he bit out tersely. 'I'm not one of your students, and I don't scare easily!'

Elizabeth doubted she could teach this man anything! As for the scared part—in his present mood, Rogan was the scary one!

Her mouth firmed. 'Look—'

'No—*you* look,' he retorted. 'Either you change your plans and don't go swimming. Or I come with you to make sure you don't drown.'

Elizabeth's chin rose challengingly even as the thought of seeing all Rogan's muscled power in only a pair of swimming trunks made her pulse quicken. Just having him standing this close to her made her pulse quicken! 'You may be in the habit of ordering other people around, but you certainly can't dictate what *I* do.'

'I can stop you swimming in what happens to be a private family cove. *My* private cove now,' he returned calmly.

Yes, no doubt he could do that… 'I'm twenty-eight years old and perfectly capable of deciding for myself what is and isn't dangerous.'

'My mother was forty-two years old—but that didn't stop her from drowning in the cove you're now proposing to swim in alone!' A nerve pulsed in his tightly clenched jaw.

Too late Elizabeth remembered that Rogan's mother had died by falling—jumping?—from the cliffs into the Cornish sea. She just hadn't realised it was the cliffs above the same family-owned cove she swam in every morning…

She grimaced. 'I'm sorry, Rogan, I wasn't thinking when I said that—'

'Save your platitudes for someone who appreciates them,' he cut in coldly. 'Are you giving up the idea of swimming this morning, or do I have to come with you?'

'You're really serious about this?' she said doubtfully.

'There's a time and a place for humour, Elizabeth, and this isn't one of them!' Rogan assured her grimly. Just the thought of Elizabeth's broken and lifeless body being washed up on the beach by the tide made his blood run cold.

Quickly followed by a surge of heat through his whole body at the thought of seeing her swimming in a skimpy bikini. All that lithe loveliness, and those gloriously shapely legs…!

'I either come with you, Elizabeth,' he insisted, 'or you don't go. It's up to you.' He folded his arms belligerently across his chest.

She grimaced. 'Not much of a choice, is it?'

Rogan didn't even bother to answer as he studied her through narrowed lids. Elizabeth looked tired this morning. Her face was pale, and there were dark shadows beneath those sky-blue eyes.

She had been very quiet last night, almost introspective, following their conversation about her father. But, as Rogan's own thoughts had been far from pleasant, he hadn't been in the mood at the time to even attempt to goad her into further conversation.

Once again he had told himself that Elizabeth Brown was most definitely not his type. She was too prim, too controlled, too serious—and, worst of all, beneath that frosty exterior he now knew that her emotions were too fragile.

His brain knew and accepted that. His body was still less than convinced!

'Okay,' Elizabeth conceded with a sigh. 'But I don't go down to the beach to dip my feet in the shallow water. I swim for exercise, not fun.'

Rogan grinned. 'Think I can't keep up with you?'

No, Elizabeth was pretty sure that he could keep up

with her in almost anything. That was the problem. *He* was the problem.

He infuriated her. He challenged her. Most of all, he disturbed her…

Her mouth firmed. 'I'll wait here for you while you go and get your towel and trunks.'

His grin widened. 'No skinny-dipping, then?'

Colour warmed her cheeks. 'Sorry to dash your hopes,' Elizabeth said dryly.

'*C'est la vie.*' He shrugged unconcernedly. 'I'll be one minute,' he promised, before turning to ascend the stairs two at a time.

One minute was nowhere near long enough for Elizabeth to collect her marauding thoughts. Especially the one where she imagined Rogan as the one swimming naked…

Rogan watched from beneath lowered lids as Elizabeth sat down on the golden sand a short distance away to pull her T-shirt over her head before peeling her jeans down the silky length of her legs, revealing that she wasn't wearing the bikini of his imagination, after all, but a plain black one-piece sports costume.

A plain black one-piece sports costume that, as Elizabeth rose fluidly to her feet, was surprisingly more sexy than any bikini could ever have been as it clung to the firm swell of her breasts, narrow waist and slender hips above those deliciously shapely legs…

Rogan felt his temperature and other things rise just looking up at her. Hell, this woman was so sexy she was totally destroying his normally unshakeable self-control!

A dip in the ice-cold sea was exactly what Rogan needed

to ease the throb of desire that was threatening to send him over the edge. Although at the moment, with his body so obviously aroused, standing up could be something of a problem!

Elizabeth gave him a puzzled glance. 'Have you decided the sea looks too cold to come in, after all?'

He raised dark brows. 'Is that a challenge, Dr Brown?'

'Could be, Dr Sullivan. Or is that Lieutenant?' She arched auburn brows.

Actually, it had been Captain… 'It's just plain Mr nowadays,' he confirmed dryly, before turning away to pull the black T-shirt over his head.

My God! There was no way Elizabeth was able to hide her gasp of horror as she saw the scars that marred the muscled strength of Rogan's torso.

There were several long puckered scars on the long length of his back that looked as if they might have been made by either a knife or a whip. But it was the ones on the front of his body that caused her the most alarm. Three perfect, tiny scars that were obviously bullet holes—one in his stomach, another in his left shoulder, and another just above his heart!

'Rogan?' Elizabeth's gaze was fixed on those scars as she fell down onto the sand beside him, raising an involuntary hand so that her fingers almost touched them. 'What happened to you?' she breathed shakily.

'Obviously, I was shot.' He gave a hard and humourless smile. 'It happens when you're a soldier, Elizabeth.' He gave a dismissive shrug.

She gave a slow, disbelieving shake of her head, a sick feeling in her stomach as she continued to stare at those scars. As she imagined the bullets ripping into Rogan's flesh!

Flesh Elizabeth could no longer stop herself from

touching as her fingertips moved tentatively over the scar above his heart, feeling the hard ridge of skin that had healed over what had obviously been a life-threatening wound.

She moistened dry lips. 'I— How long ago…?'

'I left the army five years ago.'

She shook her head. 'That doesn't answer my question.'

Rogan sighed. 'You should know by now that I don't like answering questions.'

Elizabeth swallowed hard as she looked up at him searchingly. 'Is that why someone shot you? Because you refused to answer their questions?'

He moved away from her impatiently to stand up, his expression grim as he unsnapped and took off his own jeans before dropping them on the sand beside his T-shirt.

Elizabeth made no effort to get to her feet when she saw there were yet more scars on his upper thighs. 'Rogan—'

'You know, most women find my battle scars a turn-on,' he said cynically as he looked down at her.

Those blue eyes snapped with impatience. 'Women who perhaps don't have an imagination that allows them to realise the pain you must have suffered.'

'This conversation is *over*,' Rogan snapped coldly.

'You could have died—'

'But I didn't.'

'Rogan—'

'Give it up, Elizabeth,' he growled with finality. 'Come on, I'll race you to those flat rocks at the mouth of the cove!' He attempted to distract her as he threw his sunglasses down on his towel and ran across the sandy beach to the water's edge, before turning to see if Elizabeth had taken him up on the challenge.

She was only a couple of paces behind him, those blue eyes glittering determinedly and her cheeks pink and glowing. 'The conversation *isn't* over, Rogan.'

'It is if I say it is,' he insisted.

Their gazes continued a silent battle for several long seconds, before Elizabeth finally gave a terse nod. 'Last one to the rocks has to carry both rucksacks back up the cliff to the house!' she shouted in challenge, and she streaked past him to dive smoothly into the virtually calm sea and start swimming.

Rogan remained on the beach watching her, her strokes smooth and powerful as she set off towards the rocks half a mile or so away. He wasn't in the least surprised that Elizabeth swam as she did everything else: with capable efficiency.

That same capable efficiency that had told her Rogan's wounds hadn't been inflicted in any normal combat…

'What are you? Olympic level?' Elizabeth was panting hard as she drew herself up onto the flat rock before collapsing beside Rogan. She had barely swum half the distance to the rocks before Rogan had overtaken her, and he had been sitting here for several seconds watching through narrowed lids as she completed her swim.

Elizabeth now studied him from beneath her own lowered lashes…

Wet, Rogan's hair was black and silky where it rested long and damp on his shoulders. Water glistened on his deeply tanned scarred body, and the dark hair on his chest tapered down until it disappeared beneath a pair of black boxer-style swimming trunks that clung revealingly to his hips and thighs.

The ragged heaviness of Elizabeth's breathing was suddenly no longer due to the exertion of her swim!

'Not quite Olympic level,' he answered, with a shrug of those broad shoulders.

Elizabeth eyed him ruefully. 'Just another one of those "useful" skills you learnt in the army?'

His mouth thinned. 'Yes.'

'You weren't just another soldier, were you?' she asked slowly, knowing that the skills Rogan had so far shown didn't quite match up to that role.

The scars she could see on his body had only confirmed her suspicions.

He had lowered his lids over the darkness of his gaze. 'I told you, I'm not going to talk about this any more today, Elizabeth.'

'Or ever?'

'Or ever,' he confirmed.

'Because, as you said, you would have to kill me if you did? Or because you just don't want to?'

He turned to stare out across the ocean. 'Maybe both…'

'Maybe?'

His eyes were hard as onyx as he turned back to look at her. 'Why the interest, Elizabeth?'

Her eyes widened at the accusation in his tone. 'You don't imagine that I'm trying to get information out of you for the other side, do you?'

Rogan gave a hard, humourless laugh. 'Who is "the other side" nowadays, Elizabeth? I don't know, and I'm pretty sure no one else does any more, either.'

'In other words, it could very well be the woman lying beside you…' Elizabeth said thoughtfully.

He gave her a sideways glance. 'Is it?'

'Don't be ridiculous!' She sat up to express her indignation.

'Is that what I'm being?' Rogan mused. 'Ridiculous? What did my father know about you when he hired you? Come to that, what do *I* know about you?'

She glared at him. 'That I live in London. That I teach History at a university there.'

'Those are only the obvious facts, Elizabeth,' Rogan pointed out wryly. 'Who are your associates? Your friends? What are your political leanings?'

'I don't have any political leanings— all politicians are as bad as one another, from what I can tell,' Elizabeth said. 'And my associates are highly qualified people as dedicated to teaching as I am.'

'And your friends…?'

Elizabeth shifted uncomfortably under the sudden intensity of that dark gaze. 'I have a couple of female friends from school that I keep in touch with…'

'What about men?' Rogan probed softly. 'Who do you sleep with? Share pillow-talk with?'

'Pillow-talk?' she echoed breathlessly.

'If you prefer it, post-coital conversation,' Rogan drawled.

'I don't!' Elizabeth said frowningly.

Rogan turned so that he was now lying only inches away from Elizabeth, their thighs almost touching. 'You don't prefer it, or you don't engage in post-coital conversation?'

'Both!' In spite of the coolness of the early-morning air, Elizabeth suddenly felt very warm. Because of Rogan's close proximity? Or the intimacy of their conversation?

'Is the latter because you don't have a man sharing your bed at the moment, or do you just prefer not to talk after sex?'

Her cheeks burned. 'Stop interrogating me, Rogan!'

'Believe me, it's preferable to what I really want to do!'

Elizabeth's gaze avoided Rogan's as she saw the heat that had suddenly entered those dark, caressing eyes. Instantly making her aware of how her breasts were clearly outlined by the clinging material of her black costume, the nipples pebble-hard and aching!

She moistened salty lips. 'It's probably time we were going back now—Rogan?' Her gaze was raised to his in alarm as he reached out to curve his hand about the nape of her neck. 'Rogan!' But she could only protest half-heartedly as that hand tightened and he began to draw her inexorably closer to him.

Elizabeth couldn't move, felt totally captivated by the intensity of his eyes as his gaze so easily held hers. Her lips were already moist and parted as his mouth claimed hers. First gently, searchingly. Then hungrily as he opened her lips even further at the same time as he pulled her into his heat and curved her body into his much harder one.

Her response was instant. Spectacularly out of control, and her hands moved up his chest and she clung to those wide muscled shoulders as Rogan's lips continued to devour and claim hers.

She didn't have the will-power to protest as Rogan lowered her back down onto the flatness of the rock, was too lost in pleasure as they kissed with lips, tongues and teeth. Fiercely. Hungrily. Elizabeth's hands moved restlessly across Rogan's back, tracing and caressing each and every scar in a way that seemed to increase the hunger of his mouth as it moved passionately over hers.

His hands moved to curve about the firm thrust of her breasts, the soft pad of his thumbs tracing the outline of her hardened nipples, the elusiveness of those near caresses sending rivers of expectation, pleasure, pooling between Elizabeth's thighs.

She wanted—Oh, God, she wanted…!

She broke the kiss to gasp. 'Please, Rogan…!' And that gasp became a shuddering cry as he lowered his head to claim the fiery tip through the material of her costume, drawing the nipple into the heat of his mouth and laving it with the rasp of his tongue…

There was so little clothing between them, only the thin material of their bathing costumes, but it was still too much as far as Rogan was concerned. He wanted to see, to touch, to kiss every silken inch of Elizabeth's bare flesh.

He moved his mouth reluctantly from her breast so that he could move back slightly, his dark gaze resting briefly on her flushed face before he glanced down to watch as he drew both straps of her costume slowly down her arms, pulling the material down even further so that he could bare her breasts, full and lush, the nipples a deep rose-pink, perfect in their arousal.

The skin of his hands looked dark against the pale creaminess of her flesh as he sat up to cup the fullness of both breasts, claiming those nipples to roll them, gently squeeze them between thumb and finger. Rogan felt his thighs throb in the same pleasurable rhythm as Elizabeth half sat up, her hands resting back against the rock as she thrust her breasts forward in silent offering.

Rogan groaned his satisfaction as he moved to kneel between her parted legs, and then bent his head to take one delicious-tasting nipple into his mouth even while his hand continued to lavish attention on its twin.

She was so responsive, and Rogan couldn't get enough of her as he turned his head to pay attention to her other nipple, licking, biting, sucking, pleasuring her until Elizabeth writhed against him, her breasts jutting higher so that he could draw her even further into his mouth.

His erection was thick and hard, pulsing with need, and Rogan was almost losing control just at the thought of having Elizabeth's lips on him, about him, in that intimate way.

He was breathing hard as he finally raised his head. 'Touch me, Elizabeth. For God's sake, touch me!'

Elizabeth immediately obeyed his plea, moving a caressing hand down the tautness of his muscled abdomen until she could cup the hardness between his thighs, instantly feeling the way his arousal, so long and thick, leapt eagerly, hotly, against her hand.

Rogan reached between them to push his trunks down his hips and thighs and throw them aside, his arousal jutting forward eagerly as Elizabeth's fingers closed about him and the soft pad of her thumb touched and stroked him until he hardened even further.

Elizabeth moaned softly at this physical evidence of Rogan's arousal. He was steel encased in velvet, the blood pulsing fiercely, hotly, as he swelled beneath her questing hand.

Her own body was wound so tight she felt as if there was a coiled spring inside waiting for release, and she offered no resistance when Rogan reached between them once again, this time to pull her costume down even further, over her thighs and hips, until he had discarded it completely.

Elizabeth's legs parted invitingly and she continued to touch and caress Rogan as he thrust rhythmically into her encircling fingers.

'It'll all be over if you don't stop now!' he groaned, and he reached down to remove her hand, instead nudging her legs apart so that he could move up onto his knees between them to look down at her nakedness.

Elizabeth moistened her lips with the tip of her tongue, her hips rising in invitation as her gaze remained riveted on the jutting hardness between Rogan's muscled thighs.

She cried out, her startled gaze rising to Rogan as she felt his hand glide smoothly along her inner thigh. She could see the dark passion in Rogan's eyes as he looked down at her bared thighs, knowing by the wild gleam in them, and the flush beneath his hard cheekbones, how aroused that made him feel.

Elizabeth cried out again as he touched lightly between her thighs. She was so swollen there, so aching and aroused that she knew herself to be balanced on the very edge of climax.

Rogan's gaze was hot, scorching, as he felt Elizabeth's instant response when he slowly parted the silky auburn curls, baring that pulsing nub. He used one finger to lightly stroke around, above and below that arousal, without quite touching it, drawing out Elizabeth's pleasure as she groaned and whimpered and writhed her hips in search of that caressing finger.

Rogan pushed her legs even wider apart so that he might caress her lower still, instantly feeling how she opened for him as he stroked the swollen entrance and found her hot and slick with need, her hips arching upwards in a plea for release.

A soft scream escaped her parted lips as Rogan dipped the tip of his finger inside her wet and creamy tightness, her muscles convulsing greedily about him, the soft panting of her breath telling him how very close she was to exploding.

'Not yet, Elizabeth!' Rogan slowly withdrew his finger

to resume his playful caresses. Around. Above. Below. Never quite touching…

He continued those tantalising caresses even as he lowered his head to her bared breast, once again drawing hungrily on her nipple, groaning low in his throat as he felt Elizabeth's hands become entangled in his hair as she held him to her.

'Please, Rogan!' she cried out restlessly, desperately, as her fingers tightened painfully in his hair. 'Please…!'

'Say it again, Elizabeth,' Rogan groaned against the moist heat of her nipple. 'Say my name, damn it!'

'Rogue…?' she breathed raggedly.

'Yes!' he rasped. 'Say it, Beth. Say it!'

'Rogue, Rogue, Rogue…!' Her cries became a gasping litany as Rogan kissed his way slowly down the flatness of her stomach, over the smoothness of her hips, until he reached those damp, fiery curls between her legs, when that cry became another scream as he placed his lips about her and then stroked his skilled tongue against the throbbing centre of her desire.

Elizabeth arched up to that stroking tongue as ecstasy ripped through every part of her, threatening to shatter her into a million pieces. Her muscles convulsed in an endless release as Rogan continued to pleasure her, until Elizabeth finally collapsed back weakly, completely sated.

The moment the coldness of the rock touched Elizabeth's back, she was brought back to the reality of where she was, who she was with, and what had just happened.

'I've always found regret to be a wasted emotion,' Rogan murmured dryly some minutes later, when Elizabeth made no effort to lower the arm she had draped over the top of her face.

As if not being able to see him would make all that had just happened go away!

Which was pretty ridiculous when they were both still completely naked…

Rogan moved up to lean on his elbow, looking down at her. Her breasts were slightly red from the rasp of his early-morning stubble, the nipples still engorged and dusky pink from the ministration of his lips and tongue, and those fiery curls between her legs were damp from her recent release.

He drew in a shaky breath. 'Beth—'

'I don't want to talk about this now!' Elizabeth snapped fiercely, lowering her arm so that she could glare up at him.

'Or ever?' he guessed ruefully.

'Or ever!' Elizabeth echoed as she sat up to look for her discarded bathing costume. It lay some distance away on the rock, tangled into a wet, unappealing ball.

Dear God…!

What had happened to her just now? How could she have allowed herself to completely unravel in Rogan's arms like that?

How could she have been so foolish!

'I like your hair all soft like this—'

'Don't touch me!' Elizabeth flinched back as Rogan would have reached out and touched the silkiness of her recently dried hair.

Rogan's eyes darkened angrily as his arm dropped back to his side. 'You didn't seem to object a few minutes ago when I *touched* you!'

Colour burned Elizabeth's cheeks as she remembered all too clearly the shameful way she had pleaded for his touch.

She'd been so aroused, so aching, so desperate for release as she urged Rogan to give her what she needed…

Something he had done beyond her wildest imaginings!

She swallowed hard, her gaze no longer meeting his. 'I must have been out of my mind.'

'Oh, you were,' Rogan said pointedly. 'Completely and wildly out of your mind.'

Her eyes shot furious sparks at him. 'Do you have to sound so—so damned triumphant?'

He gave an unrepentant shrug. 'It's a natural reaction in a man when he knows he's just given his woman pleasure.'

'I'm not *your* woman,' Elizabeth gasped incredulously.

'Just say the word and you could be,' Rogan drawled softly, having no idea how he would handle having someone like Elizabeth in his life, but knowing that giving this woman pleasure once hadn't been nearly enough to satisfy his own appetite for her. He wanted to make love to her again. And again. And have her make love to him, too…

The throb of his thighs ached all over again just at the thought of having the fullness of her lips about him, her tiny tongue lapping the length of him…

'For how long?' she came back challengingly.

Rogan shrugged. 'For as long as it lasted.'

'"It" being a purely sexual relationship?'

'Of course.'

Elizabeth gave a disgusted shake of her head. 'I have absolutely no wish to become the latest woman in what I have no doubt is the very long line of your conquests!' She spat the words at him as though he'd just mortally insulted her.

The coldness of her rejection was like a slap in the face after Rogan's imaginings. In which, knowing how much a woman like Elizabeth didn't belong in his world, he had wanted to take her there anyway….

'Didn't my lovemaking measure up to the "dark predator" in your book?' he taunted sarcastically.

Colour heated Elizabeth's cheeks at this reference to the book she had been reading the night Rogan arrived. After the way she had responded to him how could he even suggest that his lovemaking hadn't measured up? Making love with him had been beyond anything Elizabeth could ever have imagined it to be.

'I'm going back to the house now,' she bit out abruptly. 'Try not to get cut off by the tide, won't you?' she added with false sweetness as she rose to her feet, grabbing up her costume and holding it in front of her nakedness as Rogan made no effort to hide his admiring glance.

Rogan had no chance to make any reply as he watched Elizabeth walk away.

He sighed heavily as he fell back onto the rock, its coldness acting as a balm to the ache in his loins as he stared up at the cloudless sky.

Elizabeth obviously wanted to forget what had happened, but there was no way Rogan would ever be able to forget the way Elizabeth had caught fire in his arms just now. Her ready response to the caress of his mouth and hands on her body. The tremors of her shuddering release.

Even if he wanted to, there was no way Rogan could ever forget *any* of that…

## CHAPTER SEVEN

'DOING some late spring-cleaning...?'

Elizabeth straightened to turn and stare numbly across the room at Rogan as he stood in the doorway of the library. 'I found it like this when I came in just now.'

'Like this' was with dozens upon dozens of books tumbled haphazardly from the shelves onto the floor, until hardly any of the carpet remained in view.

Elizabeth had been dreading seeing Rogan again after the incident down in the cove earlier this morning. But coming into the library to find the room in complete chaos had put that embarrassment completely from her mind. All she wanted to do now was just sit down and cry in the midst of all this wanton destruction.

She dropped down heavily into the chair that sat in front of the desk. 'Who could have done such a thing?' She stared down at the piles of books in disarray around her. 'And why?'

'I think at this moment I would be more interested to know when.' Rogan stepped carefully over the piles of scattered books as he came further into the room.

'When...?' Elizabeth echoed dazedly.

He shrugged. 'Did this happen last night, after we had gone to bed, and we just didn't hear it? Or did someone enter the house earlier this morning while we were down at the beach?'

Some of the colour returned to Elizabeth's cheeks at his reference to 'earlier this morning'.

'Is there anything missing? Stupid question,' he instantly acknowledged as Elizabeth gave him an impatient glance. 'I was just trying to decide whether we should tell the police it was simple vandalism or theft.'

'Theft?' Elizabeth repeated breathlessly, her gaze instantly going to the glass cabinet that stood against the wall near the door.

A glass cabinet that Rogan could see stood completely empty, with both of its doors smashed. 'Is that where you put all the valuable books? The Darwin and other books you mentioned yesterday?'

Elizabeth gave a pained wince. 'Yes. I—I thought it best to keep them all together… But I just made it easier for a thief, didn't I?' she realised self-disgustedly. 'I— Do you think we should call the police?' She frowned as Rogan's earlier comment finally registered.

He arched dark brows. 'Don't you?'

'I… Yes. Of course.' She stood up again to run the palms of her hands down her denim-clad thighs. 'If you're comfortable with that?'

'If I'm— Why the hell wouldn't I be comfortable with it?' Rogan demanded.

Elizabeth could no longer meet Rogan's dark and probing gaze. 'I just thought—'

'I don't think I want to know what you thought, Elizabeth!'

he bit out. 'Did imagining I might be involved in something illegal add to your pleasure this morning?' he continued scornfully. 'Did it make it more exciting for you?'

Elizabeth felt the colour quickly drain from her cheeks at Rogan's tone. 'There's no need to be insulting—'

'Oh, I think there is,' he insisted. 'What do you imagine it is I do in the States, Elizabeth? Something illegal, obviously. Gun-running, maybe? Or selling drugs?'

'Don't be ridiculous!' she snapped uncomfortably.

Elizabeth had no idea what Rogan did or was in America; how could she, when he refused to talk about himself?

He folded his arms in front of that broad, muscular chest. 'So what else did you come up with after you had eliminated gun-running and drugs?'

She made an agitated movement. 'Stop this, Rogan.'

'No, seriously,' he grated, 'I'm interested.'

He might be 'interested', but Elizabeth was under no illusion as to the fact that Rogan was furiously angry too. With good reason…?

She moistened dry lips. 'I imagined—thought that—that maybe you're a mercenary…'

Rogan's eyes glittered as hard as jet. 'From being a soldier for my country to becoming a hired killer for whoever can pay the most money?'

When he put it like that… 'Perhaps not.' Elizabeth grimaced. 'Maybe if you were willing to talk about yourself more…?'

'And spoil all your fun?' he taunted glacially. 'I wouldn't dream of it!'

Elizabeth wasn't having fun at all! 'I apologise if I've insulted you, Rogan—'

'I can't imagine why you would think I might be insulted at being thought a mercenary?' he said.

She clasped her hands tightly together. 'I have apologised…'

'And that makes it okay, does it?' he exclaimed.

'No, it obviously doesn't make it okay,' Elizabeth accepted softly. 'I had no right to make assumptions concerning your—your present profession.'

'No, you didn't,' Rogan agreed. 'I assure you I have absolutely nothing I need to hide from the police, Elizabeth. Can you claim the same?'

She frowned at the challenge she heard in his voice. 'What could *I* possibly have to hide?'

Rogan folded his arms across his chest. 'You tell me.'

Elizabeth gave a confused shake of her head. 'I have no idea what you're talking about…'

He scowled. 'How much does a university lecturer earn, Elizabeth? Not nearly enough, I'm sure. And no matter how much it is, I'm sure you could still use a couple of hundred grand extra to put in the bank.'

'You think that *I* did this?' Elizabeth gasped weakly, her hand moving up to her throat. 'That I came back from our swim and deliberately wrecked the library in an effort to cover up the fact that I've stolen the first edition Darwin?'

Rogan's mouth thinned. 'It doesn't sound any less plausible than you thinking I'm a damned mercenary!'

No, it didn't sound less plausible, Elizabeth acknowledged numbly. Except her salary as a university lecturer wasn't her only source of income. A university lecturer was what Elizabeth was, what she did, but the money she earned doing it was nothing compared to the legacy her mother had left for her when she had died ten years ago.

But that happened to be Elizabeth's business and no one else's!

She straightened. 'I believe we've possibly insulted each other enough for one morning, don't you?'

'Oh, I don't know—'

'Rogan!' Elizabeth interrupted. 'Let's just call the police now and let them handle this investigation.'

Rogan studied her through narrowed lids, knowing by her suddenly closed expression that she was hiding something. Whether that something had anything to do with the wrecking of the library, he had no idea…

'Well, that wasn't too helpful, was it?' Rogan said frustratedly an hour or so later, as he helped Elizabeth pick up the books and check the titles before putting them into neat piles.

The police had arrived, ascertained there were no signs of forced entry, taken their report, and then left again. All within the space of that one hour.

'I did tell you that there had been several break-ins in the area recently,' Elizabeth answered him distractedly, as she checked the titles of yet more books.

'The police might stand a better chance of catching the thief if they took a little more interest in the scene of the crime!' Rogan muttered scathingly.

'We don't know if there's been a crime—except for the obvious vandalism—until we check whether or not any of the books are missing,' Elizabeth reasoned. Much as the police had said a short time ago, which was why she and Rogan were now trying to sort the books into some sort of order.

Which, Elizabeth knew, could take hours. Days. It was one thing to catalogue the books when they were in some sort of order on the shelves, another thing altogether to know whether or not any of them had been stolen when they were piled haphazardly on the floor.

'Perhaps it won't take too long to establish whether or not the Darwin is missing,' she added with a frown.

'We're more in need of your services than ever, it seems,' Rogan drawled as he resumed checking the titles of the books before stacking them.

Elizabeth gave him a sharp look. 'What's that supposed to mean?'

'It wasn't supposed to mean anything.' Rogan sighed his impatience with the increased tension between them. The break-in and their insulting conversation just now had certainly put their lovemaking in the cove onto the back burner!

Made a nonsense of it, in fact.

Which was probably as well, because Rogan was more determined than ever to get out of here, and out of England, as soon as he possibly could.

He straightened. 'I'll go and ask Mrs Baines to make us a pot of coffee. It might help us get through this,' he added dryly, before disappearing to the kitchen.

As Elizabeth distractedly resumed checking and stacking the books, she wished she could make this whole morning disappear: making love with Rogan, discovering the break-in, their conversation afterwards, the unhelpfulness of the police. A pot of coffee wasn't even going to come close to taking away the suspicion and tension that now, more than ever, existed between them.

They hadn't been acquainted with each other long

enough to really know each other. They certainly didn't trust each other.

The first might nullify the second, of course. But, as Rogan had stated his intention of leaving immediately after his father's funeral, that was never going to happen.

Which was probably as well. Elizabeth's uncharacteristic reaction to Rogan this morning—that wild, out-of-control response!—told her she knew him well enough, at least, to want to stay well away from him in future.

'I'm sorry I was gone so long, but I couldn't find Mrs Baines so I made the coffee myself—Elizabeth, are you *crying*?' Rogan probed disbelievingly as he came back into the library carrying the tray of coffee things and saw tears tracking wetly down Elizabeth's cheeks.

She raised a hand and touched her face, her eyes widening as she felt the wetness there. 'I'm sorry. I simply don't understand how anyone could have done this.' Her expression was bewildered as she stared down at the tumble of books that still surrounded her. 'Books don't harm people. They're here to provide knowledge. Entertainment. They're my *life*.' Her voice wobbled emotionally. 'My friends,' she added shakily as the tears once again fell softly down her cheeks.

Rogan put down the tray before crossing to her side to look down at her searchingly, knowing by the bruised look beneath her eyes, the pallor of her cheeks and the slight trembling of her hands that she was genuinely shaken by this whole thing.

He liked and appreciated books as much as the next man—or woman—but, as with all objects, he considered them replaceable.

Elizabeth talked about them lovingly, felt pained at their

having been tumbled from the shelves in this way. She called them her friends…

There weren't too many people in his life that Rogan trusted, but he would certainly count Ace, Grant, Ricky and a couple of other men he had served with amongst them.

What sort of life had Elizabeth led—did she still lead?—that she considered books her friends rather than people?

'Hey, it's not the end of the world.' He put his fist beneath her chin and raised her face so that he could look down at her. 'A couple of hours and we should have restored some semblance of order.'

Elizabeth was totally aware of the touch of Rogan's hand as it burned against her skin, knew she should move away, but as the darkness of his gaze captured hers, and the warmth of his body so close to hers acted almost like a narcotic, she felt unable do so.

She moistened dry lips. 'I'm sure you must have other things you need to be doing…'

He grimaced. 'Such as sorting out my father's personal belongings? Believe me, I'm in no rush whatsoever to start doing that.'

His father!

Elizabeth was crying over a few books and Rogan's father had died only days ago. That father and son hadn't been close didn't change the fact that Brad Sullivan was dead.

She stepped away from the touch of Rogan's hand. 'I'm so sorry. You must think me totally insensitive to be so concerned over a few books after you have suffered such a terrible personal loss.'

'As you said, books don't hurt people,' Rogan murmured huskily.

She *had* said that, Elizabeth recalled with an embarrassed wince. As well as crying over them. What must Rogan think of her?

That she was a sad individual. Very sad, Elizabeth acknowledged wryly.

'Who hurt you, Elizabeth?' Rogan probed softly. 'Someone you were in love with? Or just your father?'

Elizabeth had never allowed anyone close enough to fall in love with them! Which only left her father…

Her father had only wooed and married her mother because she had been a wealthy heiress. As a consequence, he had made Stella's life, and Elizabeth's, a misery. Wasn't that enough?

Elizabeth had always thought so. Which was why, even as a child, she had always preferred books to people.

She still preferred books to people!

'No one hurt me, Rogan,' she assured him dismissively as she moved to the tray of coffee things. 'How do you like your coffee?'

'Changing the subject, Elizabeth?' he taunted.

'Yes.' She made no attempt to prevaricate.

'So, no lover took advantage of you and then left you heartbroken?'

Her mouth firmed. 'Not yet.'

Those dark eyes glinted with humour. 'Are you saying *I* took advantage of you this morning?'

Elizabeth felt an icy chill down the length of her spine as she realised she should never have attempted to retaliate in that way to Rogan's mockery. 'I believe I asked how you prefer your coffee,' she said stiltedly.

'Black, no sugar,' Rogan supplied slowly, recognising that the previous conversation was over.

Even so, it had been a conversation that told him more about Elizabeth than she perhaps wanted him to know…

He had already realised from what had happened down in the cove this morning that Elizabeth was capable of deep emotion. That she normally kept those emotions firmly under control, hidden, was also in no doubt. He now also knew that she preferred the black and white aspect of the written word to any of those emotions.

Well, that was fine with him. He had no interest in Elizabeth Brown's emotions. Teasing her just now had been as much of a mistake on his part as making love with her this morning had been. One Rogan would do well to avoid in future.

'I can manage here on my own, if you have something else you need to do,' Elizabeth said as she handed Rogan his cup of coffee, and she saw the dark frown on his brow.

That frown darkened to a scowl. 'Such as?' Rogan scorned. 'There *is* nothing else to do here!' He impatiently answered his own question. 'How the hell did I stand living here as a kid?'

Elizabeth shrugged. 'It was your family home—'

'This was never a *family* home!' Rogan denied coldly. 'My mother's home, yes. My home, too, for the five years I lived here. But my father was never here; he lived in London most of the time. We were *never* a family together here. And after my mother died I didn't want to be here either—' He broke off abruptly, the flare of anger in those dark eyes as he glared across at Elizabeth telling her how much Rogan instantly regretted the revealing outburst.

And Elizabeth wondered at the reason for it…

Rogan thrust his hands into the pockets of his jeans. 'You said your own father is still alive?'

Elizabeth's expression instantly became wary. 'Yes…'

Rogan's mouth twisted derisively. 'Take my advice, Elizabeth, and put that particular ghost to rest *before* he dies and you're the one who's left with all the unresolved issues!'

Her brow cleared as she realised *this* was the reason for Rogan's anger. 'I don't have any unresolved issues where my own father is concerned,' she assured him coolly.

'No?'

'No,' she said flatly.

Rogan didn't believe that for a moment—was sure that behind her cool façade Elizabeth had plenty she could say to her father. But that reticence about her, that reserve, said that she never would.

Unlike Rogan, who had plenty he would have liked to say to his own father, and now never could…

'Fine.' He gave an uninterested shrug. 'I do have a few calls I need to return this morning, if you're sure you'll be okay dealing with the rest of this on your own…?'

'It's what I do best,' she told him dryly.

What she preferred, Rogan easily guessed. No doubt she believed that if she didn't rely on other people for anything then they wouldn't—couldn't—let her down. Rogan should understand that philosophy; apart from those few close friends, he followed the same credo.

He nodded. 'Fine. We'll contact the police again once you've definitely established whether or not those first editions are missing.'

Elizabeth chewed on her bottom lip. 'Do you really think they've been stolen?'

'Don't you?'

Well…yes, Elizabeth did think it a distinct possibility, considering they hadn't found any of them yet and the library seemed to be the only room in the house that had been vandalised in this way. But when could a burglar have got in? How had they got in?

'Let's hope not, for your sake,' she said.

'My sake?' Rogan echoed guardedly.

Elizabeth nodded. 'I realise how anxious you must be to get back to your life in New York after your father's funeral.'

Rogan gave a humourless smile. 'I assure you, the disappearance of a few books—even first editions—isn't going to alter those plans in the slightest,' he said, his strides long as he crossed the room. 'And, Elizabeth…?' He paused at the door.

She looked across at him warily. 'Yes?'

He gave a humourless grin. 'I no longer live in New York.'

Elizabeth felt a jolt in her chest. 'You don't?'

'Nope.'

'But I…' She gave a puzzled shake of her head. 'I wrote to you there.'

'And your letter was duly forwarded on to me, which is why I was a little late in responding.' He raised challenging brows. 'Are you even more convinced now that I must be involved in something illegal?' came his parting shot, before he let himself out of the library and closed the door quietly behind him.

Elizabeth didn't know what to believe about Rogan Sullivan any more. The man was a puzzle within an enigma.

He was also the only man to so completely breach—however briefly—the barrier Elizabeth chose to keep about herself and her emotions…

# CHAPTER EIGHT

'THANK you, Mrs Baines.' Rogan smiled up at the housekeeper later that evening as she put a plate of roast beef in front of him, after placing the vegetable dishes on the middle of the table. 'This smells delicious.'

'Thank you, Mr Sullivan.' The housekeeper was still very pale, and her eyes were red-rimmed, as if from crying. 'It was your father's favourite,' she added huskily.

'How's Brian nowadays?' Rogan deliberately changed the subject to the housekeeper's son, having no intention of getting involved in any sort of conversation that might involve his having to be polite about his father. Besides, he was genuinely interested. Brian was a few years older than Rogan, but the two of them had always been quite friendly towards each other during the five years they'd both lived at Sullivan House.

Mrs Baines's expression brightened slightly. 'Very well, thank you, Mr Sullivan. He lives up in Scotland now, with his wife and young baby.'

Rogan grimaced. 'That must make it difficult for you to see them as often as you would like.'

'He has his own life to lead,' the housekeeper accepted with a resigned shrug.

Rogan nodded. 'Tell him I said hello when you next speak to him.'

'I'll do that.' Mrs Baines nodded before quietly taking her leave.

'I suppose Mrs Baines will have to find new employment once you've sold Sullivan House?' Elizabeth commented as the two of them helped themselves to vegetables.

'The implication being you expect me to just throw her out into the street?' Rogan said curtly.

'It's none of my business—'

'No, it isn't!' he rasped.

Elizabeth raised reproving brows. 'She was very upset when your father died.'

Rogan's mouth twisted ruefully. 'More so than me, I guess.' He cut into the delicious-looking beef.

'That wouldn't have been difficult,' she said pointedly.

'Elizabeth, if you're trying to kill my appetite again you're going about it in exactly the right way,' he warned.

But Elizabeth was too exhausted to be deliberately provocative, after hours of checking and double-checking both the books that had been on the floor and then those still on the shelves.

She was so tired that she hadn't even bothered to change before joining Rogan for dinner.

Although even in her tired and therefore vulnerable state, she was very aware that Rogan had once again changed for dinner. The long length of his dark hair was brushed back and resting silkily on his shoulders, and tailored black trousers and a black silk shirt once again made him appear like those dark predators in the books she read…

She sighed. 'I was only attempting to make conversation.'

'Take my advice: attempt to make it about something else!' His mouth was set in a grim line as he resumed eating his meal.

'As far as I can tell, the Darwin, the Dickens and the Chaucer are all missing,' she came back tartly.

Rogan's gaze narrowed as he sat back in his chair to look across the table at her. 'That's certainly a change of subject!'

Elizabeth gave an unconcerned shrug. 'You didn't specify that I change it to something pleasant.'

'No, I didn't, did I?' Rogan eyed her appreciatively. 'So, you think they're all missing?'

'I *know* they are,' she corrected firmly. 'I've stacked and checked every book thrown onto the floor. Double-checked, in fact. I've also looked through all the books on the shelves. Again, twice. None of those books are there.'

'You have been busy,' Rogan murmured admiringly. 'Why only those books, I wonder…?' he mused as he once again attempted to eat his meal.

Elizabeth had been wondering the same thing. Admittedly, the Darwin was probably the most valuable book in the Sullivan collection, but there had been several others in the glass bookcase that were also worth a considerable amount of money. None of those books had been missing.

'Perhaps I was the one that stole them, after all?' she suggested lightly.

Rogan eyed her from beneath raised brows. 'I doubt you would have mentioned them to me at all if that was your intention. Besides, you and I both know there is no way you could ever have thrown all those other books onto the floor in an effort to cover up your crime.'

'No,' Elizabeth acknowledged heavily, only picking at her

own food, still upset by the events of the day. 'But surely your everyday burglar would have taken more than those three books?'

'Is there such a thing as an "everyday burglar"?' Rogan teased.

Her eyes flashed deeply blue. 'You know exactly what I meant!'

Yes, unfortunately Rogan did know exactly what Elizabeth meant. Which narrowed down the identity of the burglar considerably…

He shook his head. 'Just forget about it, Elizabeth.'

'Forget about it?' she echoed incredulously. 'I've just spent the entire day establishing that those specific books have definitely been stolen—'

'And I'm very grateful for your attention to detail,' Rogan cut in harshly. 'Now, can we just move on?'

'Move—? Rogan—'

'Elizabeth!' He glowered at her darkly.

Elizabeth eyed Rogan in disbelief. 'But—'

'Don't you have some more questions you would like to ask about why my mail still goes to New York but I no longer live there?' he interrupted.

She had lots of unasked questions on that particular subject. But as a means of ending their previous conversation it was rather too obvious. 'Not when I know they're questions you have no intention of answering, no,' she replied.

'You don't know that for sure.' Rogan grinned across at her unapologetically. Strangely, he found these conversations with Elizabeth stimulating. He was certainly never bored by them. Or by her…

'Okay, Rogan, let's test that theory, shall we?' she said.

'If your mail goes to New York, but you don't live there, where do you live?'

'Elsewhere.'

Elizabeth scowled. 'That isn't helpful.'

'I know.' He grinned unrepentantly.

'Those men you talked to on the phone—Ace and… Grant, was it?—who are they?'

'People who work with me, along with another man called Ricky.'

Elizabeth was holding her breath now. Rogan was still being obstructive, but even so he was answering her questions in his own guarded way. 'As what?'

'Associates.'

Elizabeth gave a grimace. 'You see.'

'I doubt you tell a man everything about yourself on a first date,' he retorted.

She didn't tell a man everything about herself on a second date either—because she usually ensured there wasn't a second date! Being here like this at Sullivan House with Rogan made it more difficult to maintain that distance.

'If anything, having lunch together yesterday counts as more of a date than dinner this evening…' Elizabeth frowned as she realised she had just completely contradicted her own version of their lunch together yesterday!

'True,' Rogan accepted. 'But it took your mind off stolen books for a couple of minutes, didn't it?'

Elizabeth was completely aware that Rogan was now attempting to divert her attention from where he lived and who he worked with by reverting back to the subject of the stolen books. And it wasn't going to work. 'Who was it you were asking Ace to make sure stayed put?'

'You're good, Elizabeth,' Rogan approved huskily. 'Very good, in fact.' He nodded appreciatively. 'You don't forget much, do you?' he explained at her questioning glance.

She shrugged. 'I simply have a methodical mind.'

'From teaching History, no doubt?'

'Probably,' she said. 'I've simply never been able to cope with chaos.'

'Like the library this morning.'

'Like the library this morning.' She nodded. 'You haven't answered my question, Rogan,' she reminded him dryly.

'Dogged too.' He grimaced. 'Have you ever watched a friend making a complete ass of themselves over someone you know is completely wrong for them?'

Elizabeth's eyes widened at the unexpectedness of his answer. 'I can't say that I have, no.'

'I have,' Rogan said heavily. 'And it isn't pretty. Which is why someone is with Ricky round the clock at the moment, in an effort to keep him away from her.'

She frowned. 'You're trying to stop this man Ricky from making a fool of himself over a *woman*?'

'*Trying* being the operative word,' Rogan drawled. 'The worst of it is, he knows she's bad for him. She picks him up and then drops him again when a better prospect comes along, only to get Ricky back again when that relationship goes sour on her. I've tried reasoning with him; we all have. He just can't seem to say no to her.' He frowned darkly.

'Did you ever think that maybe he loves her?'

'He says he does.' Rogan nodded. 'But if that's the case it's a destructive kind of love.'

As Stella's love for Elizabeth's father had been destructive…

Elizabeth shrugged. 'I admire what you're trying to do, Rogan, but you do know that in the end it will make no difference? That the moment Ricky can get away from you all he'll go back to her as soon as she snaps her fingers?'

Rogan gave her a searching glance as he sensed rather than heard the pain behind her questions. As if she spoke from personal experience…

But he could read nothing at all in the calm blue of Elizabeth's eyes. 'I would never let any woman treat me the way Vannie treats Ricky,' he vowed.

Elizabeth gave a short, humourless laugh. 'I doubt that in your case any woman would ever dare!'

Rogan remained unsmiling, aware that he had told this woman much more than he had initially intended. Because he hadn't liked it earlier when she had suggested he might be a mercenary? Possibly. Whatever the reason, he had confided more about himself to Elizabeth than she had told him about *herself*.

He looked across at her speculatively. 'So, how about returning the favour and answering a few questions yourself?'

Her expression instantly became wary. 'Such as?'

'Such as why do you spend your summer vacations working?'

Elizabeth shrugged. 'The same reason you can't wait to get back to America—I would be bored if I didn't do something to occupy my time.'

'Surely there's plenty for you to do in London? The theatre…shopping…'

'I can go to the theatre any time, and shopping doesn't interest me,' she dismissed.

Rogan gave a huff of laughter. 'I thought all women liked shopping.'

'Not this one,' Elizabeth said with a rueful smile.

Rogan already knew that there was a lot about Elizabeth that wasn't like other women. Like any other woman he had ever met, anyway…

'Perhaps we should just get on and eat now, hmm?' he suggested, and he picked up his knife and fork to resume eating the food that had gone slightly cold during their conversation.

Elizabeth did so happily, relieved not to have to talk about herself any more, and equally content with the fact that Rogan had finally talked to her about himself, and several of his friends, in spite of his obvious reservations.

'I certainly feel better now that I've eaten,' Elizabeth commented lightly, once the meal was over and she and Rogan had retired to the drawing room so that he could enjoy a glass of brandy and Elizabeth a soft drink.

'You were looking a little pale earlier,' Rogan acknowledged as he handed her the juice before sitting down beside her on the sofa and relaxing back against the cushions.

Instantly all of Elizabeth's senses were put on full alert. As if they hadn't been on alert already, after spending nearly two hours eating a meal with him!

She had found herself looking at his hands more often than she would have wished as she remembered the touch of them on the nakedness of her body earlier that day. When she had been fully aware of the spicy seduction of the combination of his aftershave and the male smell that was all Rogan.

What was it about this man in particular that made her so totally aware of him? From that silky dark hair down to his leather-shod feet?

If Elizabeth knew the answer to that question then she might have some way of fighting against it. As it was, she just had to accept that she was totally aware of him. Achingly so.

Just as she was suddenly aware that she hadn't even bothered to brush her hair before dinner. 'I feel a mess.' She raised a self-conscious hand to the spiky disarray of her hair.

Rogan turned his head on the cushion to look at her. 'If you're fishing for compliments…'

'I'm not,' Elizabeth assured him hastily.

'…then you chose the wrong man,' Rogan finished dryly.

Her cheeks felt warm with embarrassment. 'I was stating a fact, not looking for compliments.'

Rogan gave an appreciative grin. 'Nevertheless, Elizabeth, you look good whatever you choose to wear. Or not wear…' he added pointedly.

'I—' She shook her head. 'You're referring to what happened this morning?'

He gave a lazy shrug. 'I believe it's the only time I've seen you naked.'

Elizabeth gave him an exasperated glare even as the colour warmed her cheeks. 'And I believe I said I would prefer it if we never talked about this morning!' she snapped waspishly.

Rogan's lids narrowed. 'Just forget it ever happened, you mean?'

'Yes!' Her agitation was increasing by the second.

He gave a slow smile. 'What if I *can't* forget it, Elizabeth?'

'Try!'

He chuckled softly, enjoying her obvious discomfort. Why shouldn't he, when those same memories made him uncomfortable too—though in a completely different way!

Rogan really had tried forgetting Elizabeth's nakedness this morning. The way she had caught fire in his arms as he kissed and caressed her. How much he had enjoyed watching her face as she climaxed under the ministration of his lips and tongue. He'd only had to look at her again this evening, to be alone with her, to know he hadn't succeeded in forgetting anything about her. As the hard throb of his thighs now testified!

He shifted slightly on the sofa, so the muscled length of his thigh rested against her much softer one. 'As I suggested this morning, there's no reason why we can't explore this attraction between us further, and see where it takes us…'

Elizabeth scooted to the far side of the sofa. 'Explore it on your own and leave me out of it!'

Rogan gave a slow shake of his head and his gaze easily held hers captive. 'I'd much rather explore it with you,' he murmured throatily.

Elizabeth couldn't think straight, couldn't move when Rogan was this close to her. 'I— We both know this morning was a mistake.'

'Do we?'

'Of course it was a mistake,' she said. 'You have a woman back in America, waiting for you to call her!'

He raised dark brows. 'I do?'

She nodded. 'According to your *associate* Grant, yes.'

Those dark eyes narrowed as he obviously recalled the telephone conversation she was referring to. 'You really don't forget anything, do you?'

'Nothing of importance, no,' she assured him firmly. 'Besides, you and I have nothing in common.'

He relaxed slightly. 'Admittedly I don't read sexy vampire novels…'

'Will you just forget about those damned vampire novels?' She glared at him crossly.

'Difficult,' Rogan murmured, those dark eyes warmly seductive now. 'Aren't you tempted to practise some of the things you've read about?'

Her cheeks felt even warmer. 'No, I am not! They're only fantasy, Rogan,' she added. 'Not real life.'

'How do you know that if you've never experimented? For instance, I think we might both find it highly erotic if, while I was making love to you, I were to bite you on the neck.'

'Will you just stop this!' she burst out agitatedly. 'You simply aren't my type.'

'You seemed to think I might be this morning,' he reminded her mockingly.

'You took me by surprise this morning.'

'If my memory serves me correctly, I didn't *take* you at all…'

Her mouth firmed. 'You're just bored, Rogan, and looking for a diversion. Any diversion.'

'You think?'

'I know!'

'Never heard of opposites attracting?' he taunted.

'Not in this case, no.' She shook her head. 'We're just too different for this attraction to be real, Rogan. Your life appears to be complicated, in so many ways. Whereas I like stability and certainty in my own life.'

'Stability and certainty can be a little boring, don't you think?' he asked, his gaze continuing to hold hers even as he reached across to pick up her hand and lace the long length of his fingers with her much smaller ones.

Elizabeth felt the jolt of that physical connection as heat

surged up the length of her arm and into her breasts, causing them to swell achingly and the nipples to harden and throb in awareness.

Worse, she couldn't look away from their interlaced fingers, her own appearing very white and delicate against Rogan's much darker skin. She swallowed hard, before moistening suddenly dry lips. 'I like my life the way it is.'

'Do you?' Rogan was much closer now, his breath brushing warmly against her slightly parted lips. 'Do you really, Elizabeth?'

She liked this man! The way he looked. The way he felt. The way he touched her. The way she felt when he looked at her with those dark, seductive eyes.

It was all too easy at times like these to forget that he had that woman waiting for him in America…

Rogan easily read the panic in Elizabeth's widely uncertain gaze, knowing he should stop this now. Knowing, after those alarm bells had rung inside him this morning after making love with her, warning him that Elizabeth Brown could be a danger to his chosen life of solitude as well as his peace of mind, that he should never have started this teasing conversation in the first place.

The two of them were both products of what sounded to Rogan to be similar childhoods—a loving mother who had died before her time, and a father who didn't give a damn about his wife or his child. Elizabeth had chosen to deal with the pain of that childhood by channelling her emotions into the safety of teaching History, whereas Rogan had just as deliberately chosen a life that presented constant challenge and change.

He didn't want, had never wanted, any permanence in his

own life. He certainly didn't want a permanent woman—least of all a woman like this one!

Rogan released her fingers as he sat back abruptly. 'You're right, Elizabeth, you aren't my type either,' he said quietly, and stood up. 'We have the funeral tomorrow to get through.' He grimaced just at the thought of it. 'So I'll wish you goodnight,' he added distractedly, before striding purposefully from the room.

'Goodnight, Rogan…' Elizabeth murmured softly into the empty room.

A room that, without Rogan's vibrantly forceful presence, somehow seemed flat and uninteresting.

Much like Elizabeth was starting to realise she had allowed her life to become…

# CHAPTER NINE

'GRAB a plate out of the cupboard, Elizabeth, and then get the toast, will you?' Rogan prompted when she entered the kitchen the following morning, while he stood over the hob, cooking eggs and bacon in two separate pans.

Elizabeth hadn't been able to fall asleep the night before, and as a consequence she had overslept and so missed her early-morning swim. She had thought she must have missed breakfast too, when she'd entered the small dining room and found it empty of all the usual signs of breakfast.

Lured to the kitchen by the tempting aroma of bacon sizzling in a pan, she was too surprised at finding Rogan there, doing the cooking, to do anything other than what he asked.

Rogan appeared perfectly relaxed, in faded blue jeans and a fitted white T-shirt. His feet were bare on the terracotta tiles, those dark eyes sleepily mesmerising, his hair silkily tousled, and the dark shadow of stubble on the firmness of his jaw showing that he hadn't yet shaved this morning…

'No Mrs Baines today?' Elizabeth asked distractedly, as she laid out two settings on the breakfast bar after collecting the toast from the toaster.

'I found her in here crying earlier this morning.' Rogan

shrugged. 'We sat down and had a chat, and as you said yesterday she's very upset,' he said, his back towards Elizabeth as he continued to cook. 'I've suggested she take the morning off, attend the funeral with us this afternoon, and then afterwards go up to Scotland for a few days and visit with her son.'

Elizabeth's hands shook slightly as she realised that Mrs Baines's unexpected departure meant that she and Rogan were now completely alone at Sullivan House…

She moistened dry lips. 'That was…very kind of you.'

Was that hollow-sounding voice really her own? Of course it was! But her sleep had been so disturbed last night, so full of dreams of Rogan Sullivan—erotically arousing dreams!—that just the thought of the two of them being alone here together filled her with dismay.

Rogan turned briefly to give her a grin. 'I *can* be kind, Elizabeth.'

'No doubt when it suits you to be, yes,' she acknowledged dryly.

He raised dark brows. 'It didn't suit me to have to cook breakfast this morning!'

Elizabeth shrugged. 'Perhaps you should have thought of that before giving Mrs Baines the morning off?'

'I gather from that you aren't going to offer to finish cooking the breakfast?'

'I'm sure you're more than capable, Rogan,' Elizabeth came back, with saccharin sweetness. 'At cooking breakfast, anyway,' she added hastily.

'You don't have a very high opinion of me, do you?' Rogan murmured ruefully as he served the food up onto two warmed plates before carrying it over to the breakfast bar.

'I believe now is a good time for me to take the Fifth!' she joked.

'Did you just tease me, Elizabeth?' Rogan asked appreciatively as he sat down on the stool opposite hers.

Warm colour entered her cheeks, and her gaze didn't quite meet his as she muttered, 'I may have done.'

Rogan nodded. 'I liked it.'

'I shouldn't.' Elizabeth raised her eyes to look across at him guardedly. 'I doubt it will happen again.'

Rogan regarded her closely. Elizabeth was her usual efficient-looking self this morning, in a cream silk blouse, brown tailored trousers and no-nonsense brown brogues. Her hair was moussed and spiky, her make-up light and her lips glossed pale peach. Even so, there was something different about her. A softness about her eyes and the full pout of her lips that made Rogan's thighs harden and ache at just imagining them curved moistly about his.

Damn it to hell!

Rogan had spent most of the night telling himself to forget all about the prickly and complicated Elizabeth Brown. To forget the silky feel of her skin, and the erotic taste of her. That a woman like her spelt trouble for a man like him. And now, just looking at her again, he was sitting here aroused like never before!

'Eat your breakfast, woman!' he snapped, his own appetite—for food, at least—having completely evaporated in the last few seconds.

'Yes, sir!' she came back, with a mocking salute.

Rogan scowled across at her darkly. 'Would you be quite so obliging, I wonder, if I were to order you to strip naked and lay yourself open to me on top of this breakfast bar?'

he rasped stupidly, his thighs throbbing anew just at the thought of having Elizabeth offering herself to him like that.

Elizabeth knew that Rogan meant to disconcert her. And he had definitely succeeded! But she had no intention of giving him the satisfaction of knowing that he had. 'Not until after I've eaten my breakfast, anyway,' she retorted tartly, before resuming eating.

He sighed heavily. 'Elizabeth—'

'Could we just eat, Rogan?' The steadiness of her gaze met his unflinchingly.

He sighed. 'You're dangerous, do you know that?'

Elizabeth hid her surprise at this statement behind another glib comment of her own. 'No one has ever accused me of being that before.'

Rogan's mouth thinned. 'You don't have to sound so pleased about it.'

She couldn't help smiling at his disgruntled expression. 'I'm a boring university lecturer—of course I'm pleased about it!'

Boring was one thing Elizabeth Brown definitely was not, Rogan acknowledged grimly. For one thing, he never quite knew what mood she was going to be in when next he saw her—this morning's teasing was an example of that. For another, no matter how hard he tried, he couldn't get the feel and taste of her yesterday out of his head. Or his senses. In fact, just looking at her now made him want to repeat the experience.

'Let's get one thing straight, shall we, Elizabeth?' he said. 'I have some more of my father's things to go through this morning, the funeral to attend this afternoon, and then I'm definitely getting out of here.'

As if the hounds of hell were snapping at his heels, Rogan acknowledged self-disgustedly. Because there was already a danger of being snared in the trap that a woman like Elizabeth Brown could set around a man's heart and his freedom…

Elizabeth's expression remained calmly noncommittal as she nodded. 'You already told me that.'

'Well, now I'm telling you again!' Rogan scowled at her fiercely.

Elizabeth placed her knife and fork carefully against the side of her plate before reaching out to lightly touch one of the hands Rogan had clenched on top of the breakfast bar. 'I realise this is going to be a difficult day for you, Rogan…'

'Do you really?' He turned his hand over and tightly gripped Elizabeth's between steely fingers. 'And how can you possibly know that?' he scorned. 'Have *you* ever had to attend the funeral of the father you despised?'

No, she had never had to do that. Not yet, anyway. But one day Elizabeth knew she would have to do so. And, just like Rogan, she was going to hate the hypocrisy that would necessitate her being there.

Rogan watched the emotions on Elizabeth's face. She wasn't guarded enough or quick enough to hide them from him. He saw her pained expression. Her dismay. Followed by her firm resolve to do what she knew was right.

So was he.

'Tell me about him, Elizabeth,' Rogan encouraged persuasively, his fingers gentling as they became entangled with hers and he ran the soft pad of his thumb caressingly across her palm. 'Tell me about your father.'

Those blue eyes flickered briefly to his before she looked quickly away again. 'There's nothing to tell.'

'Elizabeth…'

She ran the pink tip of her tongue over dry lips. Completely unaware, it seemed, of the eroticism of the movement.

Unlike Rogan, who was aware and responded to everything that Elizabeth Brown did and said…

'Please, Elizabeth…' he urged softly.

She closed her eyes briefly, before raising her lids to stare at a point over Rogan's left shoulder, her gaze unfocused as her thoughts and emotions all became channelled inwards. 'My father married my mother after deliberately getting her pregnant.'

'Why deliberately?'

Elizabeth swallowed hard. 'My mother was—well, she was… My mother came from a wealthy family. Was an heiress. He—Leonard—wanted the life her prestige and money could give him, and so when her father died unexpectedly he—he—' She broke off to shake her head sadly. 'This certainly doesn't get any prettier in the telling.'

Rogan frowned as he inwardly processed the little Elizabeth had already told him. Her mother had been an heiress. Her father's name was Leonard Brown. Why did that name sound so familiar?

'Your mother was *Stella Britten*?' he breathed incredulously, as the information Elizabeth had given him finally began to fall into some sort of order and he remembered what else was already stored in his memory.

Stella Britten. Only child of millionaire industrialist James Britten. Which meant that Elizabeth was James Britten's granddaughter—although he'd died almost thirty years ago. Within a year of his death he had been succeeded as Chairman of Britten Industries by his son-in-law, Leonard

Brown, a playboy and serial adulterer. From all accounts a total louse to the wife who had adored him. She had begun to drink as a way of shutting out the humiliating reality of her marriage, finally killing herself instantly ten years ago, when she had driven her car into a brick wall, blind drunk. Obviously the reason Elizabeth herself didn't drink alcohol. The pallor of Elizabeth's face and the pained darkness in the depths of her eyes was enough to confirm the truth to him.

Rogan drew in a ragged breath. 'I'm sorry, Beth—'

'What do you have to be sorry about?' she came back tartly. '*You* aren't responsible for my father being the selfish rat that he is any more than I am.'

Rogan shook his head. 'I should never have pushed the subject.'

'Why shouldn't you?' Elizabeth said, as she wrenched her fingers from his to stand up and move restlessly about the kitchen. 'You thought your parents' marriage was bad, Rogan? Well, you should have tried being caught in the middle of Stella and Leonard!' She gave a deep sigh. 'The worst of it is that when I was a child I absolutely adored him—' Her voice broke emotionally.

'Beth—'

'No, let me, Rogan,' she insisted. 'Maybe if I talk about him I will finally be able to put all this behind me. It's easy to see how my mother fell for him. When I was a child my father seemed so big and strong. So incredibly handsome. A golden Adonis.' Her expression softened slightly. 'He was always laughing. Forever buying me outrageously expensive presents for no reason whatsoever. The latest toys. A pony. A diamond bracelet on one occasion, because I had said I liked the rainbow lights inside it.' She shook her head bleakly. 'I was too young at the time to realise that those gifts were probably given as a way of salving Leonard's conscience because he was such a lousy husband. He had never loved my mother. Had only made her pregnant and married her because he wanted to get his hands on the company and the money she had inherited from her own father.'

There was something else nagging at the back of Rogan's memory. Something important. Something…

Then he had it. The last piece of damning information.

Stella Britten might have been besotted with her husband, but the condition of her father's will had prevented her from actually handing Britten Industries over to him, meaning that on her death her only daughter had inherited the company instead of Leonard Brown…

Elizabeth Brown. Now Dr Elizabeth Brown. Lecturer in History at a London university…and owner of Britten Industries…

Elizabeth gave a hard, embittered smile. She knew the precise moment when Rogan realised exactly who she was: his eyes widened, brows rising, that dark gaze becoming speculative.

'Yes, I'm *that* Elizabeth Brown,' she confirmed flatly. 'Are you happy now that you know everything there is to know?' she added challengingly.

Rogan didn't look happy. Instead he looked grimly forbidding, eyes hard and glittering, his mouth a thin and angry line above a clenched jaw. 'Why didn't you tell me all this sooner?' he demanded.

Her eyes widened. 'Why should I?' She frowned her confusion. 'None of that has any relevance to my reason for being at Sullivan House.'

'No relevance?' Rogan stood up impatiently. 'You're an heiress. A millionairess several times over—'

'Actually, I'm not,' Elizabeth cut in evenly. 'I gave a lot of the money away to charity, and floated most of the shares in Britten Industries on the open market ten years ago.'

'And no doubt made a fortune doing it!' Rogan scowled across the kitchen at her.

'Well…yes,' she confirmed uncomfortably. 'But none of that changes who I am now.'

'Don't be naïve, Elizabeth,' Rogan growled. 'You're the granddaughter of James Britten—and the daughter of Stella Britten and Leonard Brown.'

'I'm *myself*!' she bit out angrily, her hands clenched at her sides.

Rogan had no idea why he was so angry at Elizabeth's disclosure about who her family were. He only knew that he was. 'You're only fooling yourself if you truly believe that! Damn it, Elizabeth, why are you wasting your time teaching History and cataloguing other people's libraries when you—'

'When instead I could be living the life of a rich socialite, like my mother did?' Elizabeth was as angry as Rogan now, her eyes sparkling like sapphires as she glared at him, two bright spots of angry colour on her cheeks. 'Attending numerous parties. Film premieres. Charity dinners.' She gave a disgusted shake of her head. 'I never wanted that. Never wanted to end up being used and abused the way my mother was.'

'She just married the wrong man.'

'And you don't think *I* would have been just as hotly pursued by every fortune-hunter in England if I'd become part of that elite crowd?' Elizabeth gave him a pitying look.

'I wanted to do something worthwhile with my life, Rogan. And teaching gives me that satisfaction.'

Rogan accepted that, but it could never change who she really was…

'Fine,' he said. 'You carry on living in fantasyland, if that's what you want to do. It still doesn't change the fact that you're James Britten's granddaughter, and worth more dollars than I'll ever see in my lifetime—' Rogan broke off, breathing hard in his agitation.

Was that really what was bothering him? The fact that Elizabeth was a wealthy heiress? That knowing exactly who and what she was put her beyond his reach?

He had never wanted her to be *within* his reach!

He was a free agent. Answerable to no woman. And he intended remaining that way.

'Oh, to hell with this!' He threw up his hands in utter exasperation. 'I have work to do.' He turned and strode towards the door.

'So do I,' Elizabeth reminded him softly.

Rogan turned to give her a cold and narrow-eyed stare. 'I guess. Until you get tired of it. Then I expect you'll revert to type.'

'What type is that?' Elizabeth interrupted swiftly. 'I was eighteen when my mother died, Rogan—the same age you were when your own mother died. You disappeared to America and joined the army as a result. Instead of living the life of luxury you no doubt imagine, *I* chose to go to university, to take my degree and then get my doctorate.'

'Where no doubt you were the only student living in a penthouse apartment and being driven about by your own personal chauffeur!'

'Do I live in a penthouse apartment now?' she challenged. 'Do you see a chauffeur driving me around?'

'You probably decided to leave him in London.'

'Or maybe I just never had a chauffeur to begin with?' Her chin was raised scornfully. 'I never would have believed it, Rogan, but you're an inverted snob!'

'What is that supposed to mean?' Those dark eyes narrowed menacingly.

Elizabeth stood her ground. 'It means that you considered it okay to mess around with the hired help, but not with an heiress!'

Rogan became dangerously still. 'Mess around with…?' he repeated softly.

'Make love to, then. Or, more correctly, *have sex with*,' she spat out scathingly. 'What's the matter, Rogan? Does my being an heiress *scare* you?'

A red tide seemed to pass in front of Rogan's eyes, blinding him to all else but Elizabeth as she faced him so defiantly across the kitchen, the spiky style of her hair seeming to add to her challenge, as did the scorn he could see in the deep blue of her eyes and that faintly contemptuous curl of her top lip.

It was the contempt that pushed him over the edge of the caution that was usually second nature to him.

Elizabeth's eyes widened as Rogan strode forcefully across the kitchen towards her. 'What are you doing?' she gasped, even as she took a wary step backwards.

Rogan's mouth twisted with satisfaction as that step brought Elizabeth up against one of the kitchen cupboards, leaving her with nowhere else to go. 'I'm going to seduce an heiress, of course,' he told her, standing so close to her that he could see the nerve pulsing erratically in her throat and the wide apprehension in her eyes. Could feel the heat of her body only inches away from his own. Smell the perfume that was uniquely Elizabeth's.

She blinked nervously. 'Rogan—'

'Elizabeth,' he murmured throatily, his gaze easily holding her wary one as he slowly lowered his head.

Elizabeth's lips parted of their own volition, even as she tilted her chin up slightly, her breathing shallow and uneven as she just stood there and waited for the fierceness of Rogan's kiss.

He came to a halt with his lips only centimetres away from hers, the warmth of his body close, so very close, but not quite touching hers. 'Say you want me, Beth.'

Her breasts quickly rose and fell as she breathed deeply, feeling much as a fawn must when caught in the mesmerising lights of an oncoming car.

'Beth?'

'Yes…' she groaned raggedly.

'Say it!' One of his hands came up to cup the side of her face and his thumb moved softly, erotically, between the moistness of her parted lips as he touched and caressed the inner sensitivity. 'Say it, Beth,' he repeated insistently.

She swallowed hard, aware she had awoken a sleeping tiger. 'I want you,' she repeated huskily. 'Yes, Rogan, I want you!' she said again brokenly, and she moved the short distance that separated their two bodies, her hands moving to the width of his shoulders even as she pressed herself against his much harder contours. 'I want you, Rogue!' she added achingly, when he still held himself back from her.

His eyes gleamed his satisfaction as he shifted slightly, the hardness of his thighs slowly grinding against hers and clearly telling her of his own arousal as his mouth finally claimed hers.

Elizabeth clung to the muscled strength of Rogan's shoulders as he kissed her deeply, hungrily, before his tongue thrust fiercely into the heat of her mouth in a rhythm that quickly had Elizabeth panting and pliant in his arms as her tongue duelled with his.

But it wasn't enough. Elizabeth wanted his hands on her. Wanted to touch him too. Wanted to caress the silken hardness she could feel pressed against the ache between her thighs. One of her hands moved between them to glide down the hard contours of his chest and stomach, down to—

Rogan broke the kiss and pulled back slightly as he captured her caressing hand and held it firmly in one of his. 'Unbutton your blouse for me, Beth,' he encouraged her gruffly.

Unbutton…? 'I can't,' she groaned self-consciously.

'Yes. You. Can,' he said, and he moved back slightly.

'Come on, Beth,' he said huskily. 'One button at a time. Slowly,' he cautioned softly, and he held Elizabeth's gaze captive by his as her shaking fingers moved to quickly unbutton the first two buttons of her blouse.

Elizabeth felt totally bereft without the touch of Rogan's mouth against her own, without the heat of his body pressed so intimately against her. Nevertheless, her hands trembled slightly as they slowly released each button of her blouse from its fastening, the air cool against the heat of her bare flesh, her nipples pressed eagerly against her lacy bra.

'Take it off,' Rogan growled, once the blouse was completely unfastened.

'Rogan—'

'I said, take it off, Beth.' The darkness of his gaze held hers unblinkingly. 'Take it off so that I can put my mouth on you,' he added.

She slowly shrugged her blouse from her shoulders and let it slide down her arms onto the floor, self-consciously aware of her swollen and sensitised breasts inside her bra, the dusky nipples pebble-hard against the softness of the material.

'Better,' Rogan grated as he easily lifted her to sit her on top of one of the work surfaces. 'Now the bra,' he encouraged softly.

Elizabeth swallowed hard. 'Do you expect me to do all the work?'

He gave a humourless smile. 'I'm just making it clear who is seducing whom.'

Elizabeth drew in a sharp breath. 'It doesn't have to be this way, Rogan.'

'Yes, it does,' he insisted, placing a hand on either side of her on the worktop and pinning her to the spot. 'I'm going to be inside you, Beth. Going to take you. Going to take you so fiercely and give you so much pleasure, over and over again, that you'll have to beg me to stop. Now, take off the bra!' A nerve pulsed in the tautness of his clenched jaw.

She should be angry with his demands. At the very least apprehensive at the fierceness of his lovemaking.

Instead Elizabeth felt the tremors in her body deepen. She was throbbing. Aching. Wanting. Needing.

She needed Rogan inside her…now!

She straightened her shoulders, the movement thrusting her breasts forward. 'Unfasten it for me.'

Those dark eyes narrowed on her fiercely for several breathless seconds, before he curved an arm about her back and released the fastening on her bra with one economical movement. He peeled the straps down her arms and threw the small lacy scrap of material onto the floor with her blouse. All without the steady darkness of his gaze so much as flickering from holding hers captive.

Elizabeth's mouth went dry as she attempted to breathe. Her skin felt hot and tight. That throbbing fire was increasing between her thighs.

She stopped breathing altogether as Rogan finally lowered his gaze to look down at her naked thrusting breasts. Knowing what he would see. Feeling how hard and full her dusky nipples were. Longing for him to do as he said and put his mouth on her…

'Rogan…' she said longingly, long seconds later. When she could no longer take the torment of having only the heat of his gaze on her. 'I want you *now*!'

Rogan raised that devouring gaze from Elizabeth's breasts, his eyes searching as he looked into her face. Her eyes were dark and hot, the pupils dilated. Her cheeks were flushed and soft. The fullness of her lips swollen and slightly parted.

Oh, yes, Elizabeth wanted him.

As Rogan had intended she would when he deliberately began this seduction.

The only problem was that he now wanted her so badly himself that he was in danger of losing control of his own body before he had so much as touched her!

He should get out of here. Away from her and from the temptation she represented.

Instead he reached out to part her legs, before placing his hands on either side of her waist and lifting her forward, hard against the bulge of his arousal. Her naked breasts were firm and so incredibly hot through the thin material of his T-shirt, and he began to move slowly against her, grinding his hardness against the full nub of her arousal.

He didn't touch her in any other way, just continued to thrust against her. Pleasuring her in that way slowly, grindingly, until Elizabeth cried out in a hot and throbbing release that almost took Rogan with her. He felt every quiver of that shuddering release as she arched into him, her head falling forward to rest against his shoulder as she rode that pleasure to the end.

Rogan was so hard now, so desperate to be inside her, that he physically ached with that need.

He moved back slightly to peel off his T-shirt before unbuttoning his jeans and discarding them, along with his boxers, supporting Elizabeth's weight as he lifted her down onto the tiled floor and stripped off the rest of her clothing.

His breath caught in his throat as he looked down at her lithe nakedness. Firm and thrusting breasts tipped by hard, rosy-coloured nipples. Waist long and slender. Hips and legs curvaceous, with deep copper curls nestled between her thighs.

Elizabeth gazed her fill of Rogan in return as he stood naked in front of her. The broadness of his powerful shoulders. The flatness of his stomach. His hard, jutting arousal between muscled thighs…

She felt weak at the knees just looking at him!

'Put your legs around me, Beth,' he instructed her as he easily lifted her back up onto the worktop.

She raised her gaze dazedly. 'What—?'

'Just do it…!' he growled.

Bewildered, Elizabeth shifted forward slightly, her hands clinging to Rogan's shoulders as she wrapped her legs about his waist, groaning low in her throat as the heat of her core now pressed against the hard, silken arousal that had already given her such pleasure.

That same pleasure flooded her again, heated her, and her neck arched in supplication as Rogan bent his head and his lips and tongue took possession of one hard and sensitised nipple, teeth gently biting. The sensations rocketed through Elizabeth's body to once again centre between her parted thighs.

She felt Rogan against her there, even as he continued to kiss her breasts, the tip of his shaft gently probing her dampness, slowly widening her as, inch by inch, he slid into her, filling her completely until she had no idea where she ended and he began. She arched her hips into him, crying out as he slipped even deeper inside.

'What the—?' Rogan stilled abruptly, his startled gaze raised to hers as he felt himself come up against a barrier that had never been breached. 'Elizabeth—'

'Don't stop now, Rogan!' she pleaded.

'But—'

'Don't stop!' Elizabeth's gaze was fierce on his, her fingers digging into the muscled strength of his shoulders, and she was the one to thrust her hips forward, taking all of him, her eyes widening slightly as Rogan tore through that barrier.

Rogan had never experienced anything like being inside Elizabeth. The heat of her. The silken perfection of her as she closed tightly around him. The pleasure that coursed through him as she once again clung to his shoulders and slowly began to move herself up and down the rigid length of his shaft.

Oh, dear God, the pleasure…!

He couldn't stop now.

He couldn't…

# CHAPTER TEN

'WHAT the hell did you think you were doing?' Rogan demanded accusingly as he pulled on his jeans and fastened them.

'What do you mean?' Elizabeth asked as she finished dressing before looking up at him, her breath catching in her throat as she took in the bareness of his chest, covered in the silky dark hair that she had caressed only minutes ago. 'I thought you were seducing the Britten heiress,' she reminded him tartly.

A seduction that hadn't turned out at all as Elizabeth had expected it to!

Oh, there had been the promised pleasure. So much pleasure that Elizabeth still blushed to think of the way she had climaxed over and over again as Rogan had promised she would. The most explosive, the most forceful, being when Rogan had joined her in a climax so fierce that it had left them both breathless and sated.

It was only now, afterwards, that she was confused. Rogan seemed so distant. So angry.

'I was your first lover, damn it,' he said harshly, even as he ran an agitated hand through the dark thickness of his hair.

Long hair that Elizabeth had tangled her fingers in only minutes ago, as Rogan had pleasured her until she screamed out loud…

She *had* to stop thinking about the intimacies they had shared. Had to concentrate on what was happening now. Whatever that was… She shrugged. 'Your point being…?'

'You're twenty-eight years old!' Rogan exclaimed.

'What does my age have to do with anything?' Elizabeth forced herself to remain calm. In control. Knowing that one of them being angry was quite enough for the moment.

Rogan shook his head. 'I didn't know there were any twenty-eight-year-old virgins left in the world!'

She grimaced. 'Perhaps there aren't now…'

His eyes glittered in warning. 'This isn't the time for your slightly warped sense of humour, Elizabeth.'

She gave a heavy sigh. 'Perhaps if you stopped making such a drama out of everything…'

'A drama?' Rogan repeated, still shocked to the core at his discovery that he had been Elizabeth's first lover. And knowing that had felt so good…!

He had never experienced anything remotely like the ecstasy of being inside Elizabeth. She had been so tight. So pleasurably, erotically tight…

'The *drama*, as you put it, Elizabeth,' he continued, 'is that I obviously didn't use any protection! Not that it's very likely that you'll become pregnant from just that one time—'

'You're right. I won't!' Elizabeth glared at him.

Rogan scowled darkly. 'What exactly does that mean?'

Elizabeth couldn't believe the two of them were arguing like this. Minutes ago they had been making love together. As Rogan had promised, Elizabeth had climaxed so many times she had lost count. And Rogan's own release had almost brought him to his knees. Now, instead of a pleasurable aftermath, a sated intimacy, the two of them were all but shouting at each other.

She gave a weary sigh. 'It means that for medical reasons I'm on the pill.'

Rogan's eyes narrowed ominously. 'What sort of medical reasons?'

'Personal ones—oh, for goodness' sake, Rogan!' she snapped as he raised dark brows. 'I'm not used to discussing such personal things with another person,' she added awkwardly.

Rogan crossed those muscled arms over his chest. 'Get used to it.'

Her glare intensified. 'About five years ago I had irregular and very painful, heavy periods and my doctor prescribed the pill. I've been on it ever since. Satisfied?' She shifted uncomfortably.

'I guess…' he muttered.

What had Elizabeth expected to happen after she and Rogan had made love? That he would fall down on his knees and proclaim everlasting love for her? That he would tell her he couldn't live without her? That he wanted her to marry him before he carried her off back to America with him?

No, she hadn't thought Rogan would do any of those things.

She had only hoped that he might…

Because she was in love with him? Oh, please God, she couldn't have fallen in love with a man whose every word and action proclaimed his need for freedom from emotional entanglement!

'Let's just leave this, please, Rogan,' she suggested huskily as his face darkened. 'It's a bad time for any sort of discussion about what happened just now, with your father's funeral this afternoon.'

'Next you'll be telling me that's the reason we made love in the first place,' he gritted out. 'A human need to reinforce our own mortality!'

'No, I won't be claiming that, Rogan,' she said quietly. 'I have no idea what happened just now. Or why it happened. It just did.' And neither Elizabeth nor her heart would ever recover from it!

'That's honest, anyway!'

Her eyes glittered angrily. 'I don't believe I've ever been other than honest with you.'

'You just forgot until today to mention that you were the Britten heiress!'

Elizabeth stiffened. 'I didn't forget, Rogan, I just don't consider it anyone else's business but my own.'

Rogan sighed. 'And to think I wondered—only briefly, I admit—if you hadn't been the one to take those first editions.'

She frowned. 'Thanks for the trust!'

His eyes glittered unapologetically. 'As far as I'm concerned trust is earned, not given. And the fact that you forgot to mention who your mother was, or that you were still a virgin—'

'Will you just get over it, Rogan?' she bit out impatiently. She was tired, so very tired, of Rogan's accusing tone. Especially when she suspected—feared—that she had fallen in love with him. 'If it doesn't bother me, I can't imagine why on earth it should bother you.'

Rogan glared at her in total frustration for several long

seconds, before turning away to run another agitated hand through the long length of his hair.

Why *did* Elizabeth's virginity bother him? Rogan had no idea. He only knew that it did.

As did the thought of any other man making love to her. Ever.

There had been dozens of women in his life these last fifteen years. In his bed. But he had never been any woman's first lover before. To know that he had been Elizabeth's, that she had never shared her body that way with any other man, that no other man had ever seen how beautiful she looked in the throes of pleasure, brought out a fierce possessiveness in him that was totally alien to him. A possessiveness that Rogan didn't want to feel. For any woman. Least of all Elizabeth Brown, the Britten Heiress!

He turned back to her, his expression guarded. 'You're right. Now isn't the right time for this conversation. You have work to do this morning, and so do I. But—'

'No buts, Rogan,' Elizabeth interrupted. 'As you said, twenty-eight is rather old to still be a virgin. And if I was going to take a lover, it was as well for me to take an experienced one, don't you think?' she dismissed offhandedly.

'You really don't want to know what I'm thinking right now!' he said.

No, perhaps she didn't, Elizabeth acknowledged wearily. No doubt Rogan was used to making love with women who knew what they were doing. Practised, experienced women, who knew how to give him the same pleasure he so satisfyingly gave them.

She would take a sure bet that none of *those* women had been stupid enough to fall in love with him!

She tried not to look disheartened. 'I'll clear away here, if you would like to get on with some work now.'

'Fine.' He nodded abruptly before bending to collect his T-shirt from the floor. 'We'll talk again later.' He turned sharply on his bare heel and left the kitchen.

The tension left Elizabeth's shoulders once she was alone.

But not for long, she guessed, well aware of the warning edge in Rogan's tone that had clearly stated he would find a 'right time' for their conversation some time before he departed Sullivan House for good.

How could she have been so foolish? So stupid as to fall in love with a man who had no intention—ever—of falling in love? With any woman…

Rogan went up the stairs two at a time, his expression grim, his thoughts even grimmer.

So far this had been one hell of a day. That early-morning chat with Helen Baines. Arguing with Elizabeth. Making love with her. The unsatisfying conversation that had followed.

And he still had this afternoon's funeral to get through yet!

Rogan came to an abrupt halt at the top of the staircase as he realised that making love with Elizabeth had made the ordeal of his father's funeral this afternoon fade into insignificance.

He could still feel the satiny perfection of Elizabeth's skin against his hands and lips. Still taste her. Still feel how good it had felt to be inside her. Good? It had been fantastic!

So fantastic that he knew he wanted her again. And again. In fact, he could imagine nothing he would enjoy more than to take Elizabeth to bed for the next day and night, and make love to her in every way he had ever fantasised making love with a woman.

Rogan, my boy, you are in above your head, he acknowledged with a rueful frown as he forced himself to continue on his way to his father's bedroom.

Well above his head. In fact, Rogan knew he was seriously in danger of going under completely and not recovering…!

Elizabeth stood in front of the damaged glass cabinet, her eyes wide as she stared at the four books placed neatly on the top shelf. The Darwin. The two Dickenses. And the Chaucer.

Either she had made a mistake, and the books hadn't been missing in the first place, or the burglar had come back some time in the night and returned the books he had stolen.

As the latter explanation was highly unlikely, that only left the first one. Also unlikely. Elizabeth didn't make mistakes where books were concerned.

Which meant there had to be a third explanation…

Although for the life of her Elizabeth couldn't think what that third explanation might be.

Did Rogan know these books were back in the cabinet?

Rogan…

Every time Elizabeth so much as thought of him she went weak at the knees. She couldn't help remembering their lovemaking—in the kitchen, of all places. She thought of how much she loved him. Of how he was going to leave her once his father's funeral was over and never come back. Maybe even later today? Oh, God…!

Rogan had made love to her like a man possessed—or a man bent on possession. And it had been good. So good.

Wonderful, in fact. Beyond anything Elizabeth had ever imagined—and much better that any of the eroticism in the sexy vampire novels she liked to read! The reality of love-making was so much more amazingly pleasurable than simply reading about it.

Her breasts still felt full and achy. The nipples sensitive from the ministrations of Rogan's hands and mouth. As for that soreness between her thighs…

Rogan had filled her so completely. So pleasurably. So excitingly! Every part of her had been alive and quivering as those waves of pleasure had surged through her.

Because she was in love with Rogan. Because—?

Busy. She had to keep herself busy, Elizabeth told herself determinedly. She had to stop even thinking about Rogan, let alone dwelling on how much she loved him.

Although she had yet to solve the puzzle of the returned books…

As funerals went, Rogan supposed his father's had been okay. Surprisingly, the church had been full. Mrs Baines had been there, of course. Along with Desmond Taylor, his father's lawyer. What had surprised Rogan was that many people who had once worked with and for his father had also taken the trouble to drive from London to attend. As had a considerable amount of the local people.

All of which had simply added to the ordeal as far as Rogan himself was concerned. To the point when he was now actually starting to feel ill, after almost an hour of accepting the condolences of people who actually had fond memories of his father. And probably wondered why it was that his son remained so stony-faced!

Mrs Baines, bless her, had risen to the occasion and announced that anyone who wished to come back to the house for tea and sandwiches was welcome to do so. Something that Rogan hadn't even thought of in his need to just get his father's funeral over and done with, so that he could leave England altogether and get back to his own life!

And Elizabeth had been there at his side during the whole ordeal, pale and dignified in a black business suit and white blouse.

'You're really one hell of a woman, did you know that?' Rogan murmured huskily on the short drive back to the house for the wake. The two of them sat in the back of the car that had been supplied for the family. 'You've been very supportive today, and I wasn't exactly pleasant to you earlier this morning,' he elaborated, as she turned from looking out of the car window to give him a puzzled glance.

Delicate colour entered the paleness of her cheeks. 'Any personal differences between us shouldn't matter at a time like this.'

Personal differences? Rogan wasn't sure they had any 'personal differences'. He still wasn't sure *what* was between them!

He knew he was grateful for Elizabeth's presence at his side today. Really grateful. In fact, Rogan wasn't sure he could have got through the whole nightmare of it all if Elizabeth hadn't warmly filled the awkwardness during the times Rogan simply hadn't known what to say in answer to some of the kind comments made to him about his father.

It had come as a total surprise to him how much his father had been involved in the local community in the years since his retirement. How much affection and respect he was still held in by the people he had worked with.

'Nevertheless, I'm grateful.' Rogan reached out and laced his fingers with Elizabeth's as her hand rested on her lap. 'I wasn't so hot, but both you and Mrs Baines came through for my father today.'

Elizabeth warned herself not to read anything into Rogan taking hold of her hand in this intimate way. He was just expressing his gratitude for her support today. Which made absolutely no difference to the slight trembling of her fingers at Rogan's lightest touch, or the tide of physical tension that suddenly flared between them.

She moistened peach-glossed lips. 'Rogan, I know it was Mrs Baines who took the books.'

A shutter came down over the darkness of Rogan eyes, his expression suddenly totally noncommittal. 'Sorry?'

Elizabeth gave a rueful smile. 'Mrs Baines was the one who took the first editions.'

He released her hand abruptly, his gaze watchful. 'I have no idea what you're talking about.'

'I'm not expecting you to confirm or deny it, Rogan,' Elizabeth assured him huskily. 'Mrs Baines came over to the house before lunch, and the two of us talked as we prepared sandwiches for the people coming back this afternoon. She told me—explained why she had done it. That at sixty she didn't think she would find another housekeeping job. That she was frightened of being poor in her old age, and had imagined she could sell the books. That she had heard the two of us talking about the books, how much they were worth, and had thought the burglaries in the area lately would hide the fact that she had stolen them.'

Rogan's expression was grim. 'As you said, I have no intention of confirming or denying what you've just said.'

Elizabeth nodded. 'I—I just wanted you to know that I admire the way you dealt with the situation when she made her confession to you earlier this morning. Mrs Baines is so grateful to you for reassuring her that your father arranged a pension for her in his will.'

Rogan nodded abruptly. 'It was the least I could do in the circumstances.'

Elizabeth smiled, sure that Rogan had been surprised several times today at the warmth and affection in which his father had been held by people. 'I'm not sure if this is a good time or not, Rogan, but I—I think I should tell you that I have decided to leave Sullivan House later this evening.'

'What?' Rogan exclaimed as he turned sharply in his seat to look at her. 'Because of what happened this morning?' he bit out grimly.

'No, not because of that,' she denied ruefully, the warm colour back in her cheeks. 'Rogan, whatever differences there were between your mother and father—and those differences were surely personal to them—it's been made obvious to me today, and to you too, I believe, that other people didn't see your father the way you did, that they held him in great esteem—'

'Never heard the saying "street angel, fireside devil"?' he snapped, stung by the criticism he sensed behind her comment.

'Yes, I've heard it,' Elizabeth confirmed softly. 'And that may or may not be true of both your own father and mine. But I can't forget what you said to me yesterday about dealing with the unresolved issues between my father and myself before it's too late. The funeral today, with all those people who have fond memories of your father, has shown me that I need to know, to find out for myself what sort of man my father really is. Before it's too late,' she reminded him gently.

Rogan's mouth compressed. 'The implication being, I suppose, that *I* left it too late to find out what sort of man my own father was?'

Elizabeth gave him a sympathetic look as she shook her head. 'Not everything is about you, Rogan.'

He scowled fiercely. 'I know that, damn it.'

'Then please try to understand that I have to do this—for my own peace of mind, if nothing else.'

Rogan did understand. He even admired what Elizabeth was proposing to do. He had just been totally thrown by her announcement that she intended leaving Sullivan house later today…

Which was pretty stupid when Rogan already knew he had no intention of staying on there any longer than he absolutely had to. That he would be leaving there himself tomorrow. Or at the very latest the day after that.

But the thought of Elizabeth leaving, of never seeing her again, disturbed him more than he could ever have imagined…

'Fine,' he accepted offhandedly. 'Go. But I hope you're prepared to accept that your father just may be every bad thing you ever thought he was!'

'Believe me, I do accept that, Rogan.' She gave a rueful smile. 'Obviously my mother and father weren't good for each other. But, as I told you before, I didn't know until I was old enough to realise that. I remember my father as being full of fun, always laughing, and very loving towards me when he was at home. Possibly because of the lack of love in his relationship with my mother—I don't know.' She shrugged. 'But which came first, I wonder? My mother's drinking? Or my father's affairs? I was a child, so how could I possibly know or be in a position to act as his judge and jury?'

Had Rogan acted as judge and jury to his own father…? Hell, yes. After his mother had taken her own life, he had most definitely judged his father! But he was an adult now, and not the emotional teenager he had been when he'd left Sullivan House all those years ago. Was his judgement still the right one? Or had it been as flawed as Elizabeth now felt perhaps her own had been of her own father?

Whatever the answer to that question was, Rogan certainly didn't feel like thanking Elizabeth for putting these doubts in his own mind!

'Maybe I'll see my father again and still be filled with the same anger I've felt towards him for so many years,' Elizabeth continued ruefully. 'And maybe I won't…' Her expression was wistful.

Rogan looked at her thoughtfully. 'That's a pretty gutsy outlook.'

'It may prove to be a very stupid one.' She laughed softly. 'But I have to at least try.'

Rogan had to admire her courage.

At least he would have admired Elizabeth's courage if he didn't still feel so confused by his own anger at the thought of her leaving here later today.

Leaving *him*!

The car finally pulled up to the house, and other cars with guests who had taken Mrs Baines up on her offer of tea and sandwiches after the funeral were already starting to pull in behind.

Elizabeth looked at him sympathetically. 'Are you ready to face them again?' she asked.

'Not really, but I suppose I'll have to,' he replied. 'Hopefully it won't go on too long.' And, with that, he took a deep breath and opened the car door.

# CHAPTER ELEVEN

'ROGAN?' Elizabeth said softly.

He made no move to acknowledge her presence as she stood hesitantly in the bedroom doorway. He simply stood as still as a statue in the middle of the room where she had finally found him. He had disappeared straight after talking with his father's lawyer, once the other funeral guests had left.

'Rogan, what's wrong?' Elizabeth pressed.

His expression was grim, and there was a slight pallor to his tightly etched features. His eyes were so dark and unfathomable that Elizabeth couldn't help but feel concerned about him.

'The louse!' Rogan finally grated harshly, his fingers crushing the letter he held in his hand.

'What are you talking about?' she exclaimed.

'You were right and I was wrong, okay?' He turned on her fiercely, dark eyes blazing.

She looked puzzled. 'I don't understand.'

'Take a look around you, Elizabeth,' Rogan said. 'What do you see?' he prompted angrily, already knowing exactly what she would see. What she couldn't fail to see!

Photographs. Dozens—no, hundreds of them, on every

conceivable surface in what had once been his mother's bedroom. Several of them featured Rogan himself, from babyhood to a young man. But most of them were of Rogan's mother, Maggie. A dark-haired, dark-eyed beauty who smiled so innocently into the camera.

Every family photograph that had ever once adorned the rest of the house and many more that hadn't were all meticulously framed and arranged. On the dressing-table. The bedside tables. Even the walls! Everywhere he looked, Rogan was presented with likenesses of his happily smiling mother.

The place was like a shrine!

There were even fresh flowers in a vase on the dressing table. Yellow roses. His mother's favourite blooms. Looking less than their best now. Which wasn't surprising, considering that the person who had tended them had been dead for over a week now.

Bradford Lucas Sullivan.

Rogan's father.

Maggie's husband.

'How could he?' Rogan ground out fiercely. 'All this time I blamed him. Thought— Believed— *Hell!*' His jaw was clenched so tightly it ached.

Elizabeth didn't know what to say. Or if she should say anything at all.

The bedroom was so feminine, with its lace drapes about the four-poster bed, the floral wallpaper and cream and gold décor, that it had to have been Rogan's mother's. Was *still* Rogan's mother's, in fact. Every surface was free of dust, and there was a deep blue gown draped across the bedroom chair, as if ready for its owner to slip into. Perfume and make-up bottles stood on the dressing table. Even the hairbrush had several strands of long dark hair still entangled in its bristles.

This room, the roses, all those framed photographs, were a monument to someone who had been deeply loved.

Elizabeth shook her head. 'I don't understand,' she repeated huskily.

Rogan's mouth twisted grimly. 'Neither did I. Not until I read this.' He held up the letter he had seconds ago crushed in his hand. 'I told you my father knew exactly how ill he was, and he—he left this letter with his lawyer, for me to read. After his funeral, if I'd bothered coming back for it. Or to be forwarded on to me if I didn't,' he added bleakly. 'Read it if you want.' He threw the letter down on the bed before striding across the room to stand in front of the window, the rigidity of his back turned towards her.

Elizabeth wasn't sure that she did want to read the letter that Brad Sullivan had left for his son to read after his death, feeling as if she would be intruding on something very personal between father and son. Too personal, surely, for a third party to become involved in?

Even a third party who had made love with Rogan that morning…!

She grimaced uncomfortably. 'I'm not sure that I should, Rogan…'

'Why not?' He turned and faced her. 'Wouldn't you like to know how wrong I've been all these years? About everything, it seems.'

He had been wrong about his father. About his mother. Just wrong, wrong, *wrong*!

He strode back to snatch up the letter, smoothing out the creases before beginning to read out loud. '"My dear

Rogan… My deepest regret is that you and I have been estranged all these years—"'

'Rogan, I really don't think—'

'"But it couldn't be any other way,"' Rogan continued relentlessly. '"Not without tarnishing memories of someone we both loved so dearly. Better by far, I decided long ago, that you think badly of me than of her. Your mother was, and always will be, the dearest love of my life. I fell in love with her the day I met her, and be assured I remained in love with her until the day I died. Hopefully the two of us are together again now. I sincerely hope so. These years without her have been harder to bear than you could ever imagine. Harder even than my estrangement from you, Rogan. Perhaps now you're older you might understand why it had to be this way? I sincerely hope so. For my part, I must take equal responsibility for any difficulties that your mother and I encountered during those years after we relocated in England. I was always so busy working, often not even managing to return to Cornwall for the weekends, and as such left Maggie alone and lonely far too much. In such circumstances, mistakes happen. Faced with the truth of those mistakes, we have the choice of beginning again, of forgiving and forgetting, or relinquishing the one we love most in the world. I chose to forgive and forget."'

Rogan looked up at Elizabeth. 'Don't you see? *He* was the one who chose to forgive and forget what she did, not the other way around.'

Yes, Elizabeth did see. Only too well. And her heart ached for all three of them. Maggie as well Rogan and Brad.

Because, whether he had intended it or not, Brad's letter revealed that he wasn't the one who had had an affair during his marriage. That, although Brad had forgiven and forgotten, it had been Maggie who was unable to live with her own guilt…

The next paragraph of the letter clearly showed that Brad hadn't intended his son to know that. '"But perhaps I have said too much,"' Rogan continued reading flatly. '"My only wish in writing you this letter, Rogan, is to let you know how very much your mother and I have loved you, will always love you, and how proud we are to call you our son. Always, your loving father."' Rogan's voice broke emotionally as he came to the end of the letter. 'Damn him. Damn, damn, *damn*! Why couldn't he have told me all this before he died and given me a chance to reconcile with him?'

Elizabeth didn't know what to say. In view of the doubts she had expressed earlier, concerning her judgement of her own father, what could she say that wouldn't sound like either triteness or possibly another rebuke?

Rogan felt as if he had a vice wrapped about his chest, preventing him from breathing. Preventing him from doing anything but reliving every moment of that last terrible argument with his father fifteen years ago, the accusations he had made, and all the years of neglect and estrangement since.

And he had been wrong. So very, very wrong!

Something he would have to deal with in the same way his father had all these years. Alone.

His expression was bleak as he looked across at Elizabeth and saw tears of sympathy swimming in those deep blue eyes. 'I presume you're packed and ready to go?' he asked.

She looked startled. 'I… Are you going to be all right, Rogan?' she questioned concernedly.

It was a concern Rogan didn't feel able to deal with right now. He had far too much thinking and soul-searching to do first. 'Why shouldn't I be all right?' he retorted. 'Every belief I've ever had has just been shattered into a million pieces—but, hey, it doesn't matter, does it? As my father said, we all make mistakes, right?'

Elizabeth was well aware that Rogan was being deliberately flippant in an effort to hide the depth of the pain he was feeling at learning the truth behind his mother's death. That it was his way of shielding his real emotions.

If only things were different between them. If only Rogan loved her as she loved him. Then Elizabeth might have been able to go to him. To take him in her arms. To comfort him. To hold him as he expressed all the grief he must be feeling from learning the truth.

Instead of which they were simply two people, forced together by circumstances, who had been intimate together only once. And Rogan couldn't have made it any clearer than with that 'packed and ready to go' remark that he would rather forget that intimacy had ever happened.

'Right,' she agreed hollowly. 'I haven't packed yet, but I'm just about to.' She answered his earlier question before turning away, only to pause and turn back again. 'If you should decide some time in the future that you want to continue having the library catalogued I can recommend someone…?'

'It's too soon at the moment for me to know what I'm going to do—either with this house or the library,' Rogan said.

He looked so bleak. So much in pain. So alone. It was all Elizabeth could do not to run across the room and take him in her arms. A comfort Rogan was sure to reject…

'It was just a thought.' She nodded. 'Perhaps you would prefer it if I didn't bother you again before I leave?'

'Bother me?' Rogan repeated incredulously. 'Elizabeth, you've *bothered me* since the moment we first met!'

'I'm sorry…'

'So am I,' he said. 'You'll never know how sorry!'

There was nothing more to be said, Elizabeth realised heavily.

Rogan was totally preoccupied with his feelings towards his father, and Elizabeth would be leaving shortly.

It was over.

Whatever 'it' had been…

'I'm coming with you.'

Elizabeth looked up from completing her packing to see Rogan leaning against the doorframe into the bedroom that had been hers for the duration of her stay at Sullivan House, both his thumbs hooked into the pockets of his faded jeans. 'I beg your pardon?'

Rogan straightened to stroll further into the bedroom. A bedroom that was now clean and tidy and totally devoid of any sign that Elizabeth had ever been there. 'I said I'm coming with you.'

She stared back at him blankly. 'Coming where?'

'I have no idea,' he answered. 'Wherever it is your father lives, I guess.'

'What are you talking about?' She gave a perplexed shake of her head.

As well she might, Rogan acknowledged ruefully. He hadn't exactly been polite to her an hour ago, when she'd come and found him in his mother's bedroom. But he'd had every reason not to be feeling polite at the time! He just shouldn't have taken out his frustration over a situation that couldn't be changed on Elizabeth…

Rogan still found it hard to accept what his father had done after his mother had taken her own life fifteen years ago. The secrets he had kept all those years in an effort to protect the wife he had loved so deeply, causing years of estrangement between himself and his son that Rogan could never take back.

But as he had sat in his mother's bedroom, thinking of all those things, as he had grieved for all those lost years, it had slowly dawned on Rogan that his father hadn't just been protecting Maggie's memory by keeping those secrets, he had been protecting Rogan too. He had allowed Rogan to keep his treasured memories of his beautiful mother. At great cost to Brad himself.

Human frailties. They all, every one of them, had human frailties.

His father's had been to love Maggie so much that he would have done—and had done—anything to protect her memory. Rogan's had been to put his mother on a pedestal and refuse to admit or acknowledge that she could ever have done anything wrong. Choosing to blame his father for everything rather than ever seeing any fault or blemish in his mother. And Maggie, so warm and charming, had been so guilt-ridden over her own human frailty that she had taken her own life rather than continue to live with it.

Once Rogan had acknowledged and accepted all of those things, he had also realised that Elizabeth might possibly be opening up a can of worms for herself with her decision to go and visit her own father.

'I'm coming with you to visit your father, Elizabeth,' he repeated firmly.

Elizabeth blinked. 'I— But…why?' she finally managed to ask.

Rogan's mouth compressed. 'It's too much to expect that we've both been so wrong about our fathers, and I think someone should be there to help you keep it together if your own father turns out to be as bad as you always thought he was.'

Why on earth would he want to do that for her? Elizabeth wondered. It didn't make any sense to her—but, then again, when had Rogan ever made any sense to her?

Never, she acknowledged ruefully. But she had fallen in love with him anyway!

She shook her head. 'I really don't think that's necessary, Rogan. My father lives in Surrey now—hours and hours' drive away from here.'

'Believe me, at this moment a drive to Surrey sure beats staying here,' he drawled.

Ah. Rogan's offer had to do with the fact that he had no wish to stay on alone at Sullivan House, surrounded by memories of his own parents…

'It's very kind of you to offer, Rogan—'

'You were there for me today, Elizabeth,' he interrupted. 'I intend returning the favour, that's all.'

Was that really all his offer was? Elizabeth wondered. Of course it was! Much as she might wish it were otherwise, that Rogan was as loath to part from her as she was from him, she would only be fooling herself if she tried to read anything more into it.

She shrugged. 'I'm pleased to have been of help to you.'

'Of course you are,' Rogan said. 'Now let me do the same for you, hmm?'

Elizabeth had been alone too long, made her own decisions for too many years, to be able to accept anyone's help unquestioningly or willingly.

Even Rogan's? Yes, *especially* Rogan's! He had breached her defences in a way that no other man ever had. Had made love to her in ways Elizabeth had only read about in books. Better by far to make a clean break from him, and what she felt for him, when she left Sullivan House.

'Besides, if it's as far as you say it is, I can do some of the driving for you,' Rogan added determinedly, as he sensed Elizabeth was about to voice further protest.

Protest that he could have told her would be a complete waste of her time and energy; he had decided he was going with Elizabeth to see her father, and as far as he was concerned that was an end to the subject!

'Rogan, I'm perfectly capable of driving myself wherever I need to go.'

'For God's sake, give it up, Elizabeth,' he rasped impatiently. 'Just accept that you've met someone who's as stubborn as you are!'

Her eyes widened. 'My refusal of your offer to accompany me has nothing to do with being stubborn.'

'No?' he challenged. 'Then what *does* it have to do with?'

Delicate colour entered her cheeks even as she glared across at him mutinously. 'You can't salve your conscience by forcing your help on me—' She broke off abruptly, her eyes wide, her breasts quickly rising and falling in her agitation, hands clenched at her sides.

Rogan became very still. 'What, exactly, do you

suppose I should have a bad conscience about, Elizabeth?' he asked quietly.

She looked flustered. 'Your mistake about your father, of course.'

'Really?' he pressed.

The colour deepened in her cheeks. 'Yes, really!'

'Liar,' Rogan murmured, eyes narrowing shrewdly. 'Do you regret what happened this morning?'

Of course she regretted what had happened this morning! Just as she regretted falling in love with this man when she knew he was never going to love her back!

'Let's not cloud the issue by talking about this morning,' she dismissed briskly.

'What issue is that?' He once again hooked his thumbs into his jeans pockets.

Elizabeth eyed him with frustration as she realised she was becoming distracted herself. But did Rogan *have* to be so darkly handsome? Did he *have* to be the one man who had managed to force himself past the barrier she had years ago erected so carefully about her emotions?

She scowled. 'That I do not need you to accompany me when I visit my own father!'

'Fine,' he bit out tersely. 'I'll just come along for the ride, then, and wait outside in the car while you go in and talk to him.'

'You—'

'Surrey is probably a very nice place to visit this time of year,' Rogan continued conversationally.

Elizabeth glared at him. 'Cornwall is nicer!'

He gave an unconcerned shrug. 'I've seen Cornwall. I've never been to Surrey.'

Rogan really was determined on coming with her, she realised in frustration.

And, deep inside herself, despite her misgivings, she was secretly relieved that she didn't have to say goodbye to him just yet…

She wished she *never* had to say goodbye to him!

# CHAPTER TWELVE

'SO NOW, along with the rest of the guys in my unit who survived that last mission, I run my own business in Washington called RS Security,' Rogan revealed.

He had been talking without pause for half an hour now, ever since Elizabeth had given him the directions for driving to London. In fact, he hadn't stopped talking, about everything and nothing, since they had left Leonard Brown's house in Surrey.

All in an effort to give Elizabeth the time she needed to decide how she felt about that visit to her father…

'The name RS Security covers a multitude of sins,' Rogan continued. 'Business and house security. Computers too, of course. Retrieving lost dogs…'

'*Retrieving lost dogs*?' Elizabeth repeated disbelievingly.

Rogan shot her a grin; it was the first time she had responded to anything he had said since they got back on the road. 'Well…maybe not lost dogs so far,' he conceded lightly. 'But if someone asked I'd probably do it.'

Elizabeth was well aware of what Rogan was doing—knew he was attempting to distract her by talking about anything but the visit she had just made to her father.

At best, it had been a stilted visit. At worst, it hadn't served to vindicate her father of any of the things Elizabeth had believed concerning his disastrous marriage to her mother.

What it had achieved, however, was to show her that her father had more than met his match in his second wife, Cheryl. Blonde and beautiful, and twenty years younger than her husband, Cheryl obviously kept the wayward Leonard on a very tight leash. So much so that Elizabeth doubted her father ever had the time or the opportunity to even think about straying!

Seeing her father again had helped Elizabeth to view him through the eyes of an adult, rather than the hurt child she had still been ten years ago…

Oh, Leonard was still handsome. Still charming. Still something of a rogue. Still totally engrossed in his own needs rather than anyone else's. In fact, he was still everything that had made him such a disaster of a husband for Elizabeth's mother.

But maybe if her mother had been more like Cheryl—forceful, confident of her own attributes, strong enough to go after the man she wanted and keep him—then the marriage might have turned out differently.

Leonard was still all the things Elizabeth had ever thought him to be. But most of all, he was just weak. A man who for years had fed his own ego by having affairs with numerous other women.

It was disappointing, but at the same time this evening's visit had been a successful one as far as Elizabeth was concerned. It had freed her, and her emotions, in a way she would never have believed possible. It had wiped out the anger and resentment that had coloured her own life and decisions for so long. Now she just pitied her father for the weak and foolish man he undoubtedly was.

Unlike Rogan, so strong and confident of himself, who was everything and more that Elizabeth could ever want in a man…

One thing Elizabeth had definitely learnt from this visit to her father was that she wasn't about to allow the man she wanted to just walk out of her life. At least, not without first telling him how she felt about him.

'So.' She turned in the passenger seat to look at him as he sat slightly cramped behind the wheel of her Mini. 'What it all comes down to is that you're not such a bad-ass as you would like everyone to believe you are!'

'Not such a *what*?' Rogan gave a disbelieving laugh as he shot her a sideways glance.

'Bad-ass,' Elizabeth repeated lightly. 'An American term. It means—'

'I know what it means, Elizabeth—I'm American, remember?' he pointed out. 'It just isn't a phrase I had ever expected to hear coming out of the mouth of the learned Dr Elizabeth Brown!'

She shrugged. 'I watch television programmes from America, just like everyone else.'

'And read scary vampire books…'

'*Sexy* vampire books,' Elizabeth corrected ruefully. 'If we're going to talk about them, we may as well be accurate.'

'Oh, I'm all for accuracy. What do you mean, I'm not such a bad-ass as I like everyone to believe I am?' Rogan asked curiously.

She'd got his attention, Elizabeth recognised with quiet satisfaction. 'Number one.' She held up her first finger. 'When you realised what Mrs Baines had done you quietly and efficiently set about putting the situation to rights by telling the police we had now checked thoroughly and nothing was missing after all.'

'Thanks for saying I was efficient, at least.' Rogan grimaced.

Elizabeth smiled, unperturbed. 'Number two. I'm beginning to suspect your claim that your father had arranged in his will for a pension to be paid to his aged housekeeper was not entirely truthful.'

Rogan's mouth tightened. 'No doubt he would have done if he had thought of it.'

'No doubt.' Elizabeth nodded confidently. 'Number three—'

'Exactly how many numbers are there going to be?' Rogan cut in.

'Oh, quite a few,' she teased.

He nodded. 'Then I suggest we find somewhere to stop and eat while you go through them. We've been travelling most of the day. Your father—who I noticed called you Liza!—and your stepmother didn't seem inclined to invite us to stay for dinner, and I'm starving.'

As a means of changing the subject it was pretty effective, Elizabeth allowed—she was feeling rather hungry herself. 'No problem.' She nodded. 'There's a rather good Chinese take-away if you turn right at the next corner.'

'How do you know that?' Rogan demanded as he took the appropriate right turn and instantly saw the Chinese take-away on the left-hand side of the road.

'I live just half a mile away from here.'

Rogan gave her a sharp glance once he had parked the car in front of the take-away. 'The directions you gave me earlier were to *your* place?'

Elizabeth raised auburn brows. 'Do you have a problem with that?'

Yes, Rogan had a problem with that!

Driving with Elizabeth to visit her father was one thing—although she seemed to be bearing up under the strain of that disappointment far better than Rogan had expected she might. In fact, Elizabeth seemed quite perky, considering her father was definitely a rogue and her stepmother was a beautiful harridan, but going back to Elizabeth's apartment with her definitely hadn't been in his plans!

Although he wasn't absolutely sure what his plan had been when he'd insisted on accompanying Elizabeth to Surrey…

'Just relax, Rogan,' Elizabeth teased as she moved efficiently about the comfortable kitchen, collecting plates and flatware to go with the Chinese food they had brought in with them.

Elizabeth's apartment had come as something of a surprise to him, Rogan acknowledged as he absently helped put the cartons of food on the breakfast bar. As she had assured him, it wasn't a penthouse apartment. Neither was it in a secure and classy apartment building in a prestigious part of London.

Instead, Elizabeth had the ground-floor apartment in a converted three-storey Victorian-style house. Admittedly the rooms were big and spacious, with high ceilings, but they were also old-fashioned, and the furnishings were old and comfortable rather than expensively modern.

All in all, Rogan decided he liked it.

Although he still wasn't sure about being in Elizabeth's apartment with her. Especially an Elizabeth who somehow seemed far less prickly and defensive than she usually was…

Elizabeth eyed Rogan quite openly as the two of them sat either side of the breakfast bar and began to eat. Rogan slouched slightly even as he shot her looks from beneath long, dark lashes that were guarded to say the least.

Had she unnerved him by bringing him to her apartment? She certainly hoped so!

'So, I was thinking of maybe giving my father some of the Britten money,' she said brightly. 'What do you think?'

Rogan straightened his back, dark brows raised. 'I think that's your business and no one else's,' he finally answered.

She shrugged. 'I'm asking you for your opinion.'

He frowned. 'Why don't you get back to your numbers while I have a think about that?'

Elizabeth continued to look at him for several long seconds before slowly nodding. 'Okay. We had got up to number three, I believe…?'

Rogan gave a hard smile. 'Both you and your methodical brain know that we had.'

'Yes.' She smiled. 'But I was just checking to see if you knew too.'

'I know, okay?'

Elizabeth's smile deepened. 'Right. Number three.' She held up her third finger, her expression once again serious. 'You were in the army, transferred to Special Ops eight years ago, but became sickened by the whole thing when most of your unit was wiped out five years ago, during a mission that went terribly wrong. You resigned from the military after that, along with the five other men who survived. The six of you moved to New York for a while, but moved back to Washington three years ago.'

'You *were* listening to me in the car earlier, after all,' Rogan acknowledged softly.

'Oh, I was listening to your every word, Rogan,' she assured him. 'Your scars…'

'A little memento of that last mission,' he confirmed.

She nodded. 'What happened?'

'I'm really not allowed to talk about it. But what I will say,' he added, as Elizabeth grimaced, 'is that mistakes were made. Bad intel, maybe. Whatever the reason, we were ambushed, and half of my men were killed before we got anywhere near completing our mission.'

'And the other half, Ace, Grant and Ricky included, now work for you in Washington?'

'You really do have a methodical brain, don't you?' Rogan murmured admiringly. 'They work *with* me, not for me.'

'At RS Security.' Elizabeth nodded. 'Ricky is number four on my list.'

Rogan's brows rose. '*Ricky* is? Why?'

'You care enough about him to try and stop him from chasing after a woman you know is bad for him.'

'It's what any friend would do.'

'No, it isn't,' Elizabeth contradicted gently. 'People don't care about other people in that way any more, Rogan. It's all me, me, me. But you care about Ricky.'

'He's watched my back on more than one occasion,' Rogan said.

'And now you're watching his.'

'Move on to number five, Elizabeth!'

'The woman who was trying to contact you through Grant a few days ago…' Elizabeth was willing to let the subject of Ricky go if that was what Rogan preferred. If it made him uncomfortable to admit he cared about the men who he worked with. But she wasn't going to give up on the rest of this conversation. 'I thought she was— Well, I assumed she was some woman you're involved with in New York. When I thought you still lived in New York, that is,' she added.

'You mentioned something like that before.' Rogan shook his head. 'Meg Bailey is a piranha who'd stab you in the back rather than stop you from drowning. I'd as soon bed a crocodile as I would her!'

'I get the picture, Rogan,' Elizabeth assured him with a soft laugh. Relieved beyond measure that Meg Bailey wasn't what she had thought she was. 'So who is she, if she isn't your girlfriend?'

'She works for Langley, the company who issued our assignments.'

'She's one of the people who let you down five years ago?'

'She is,' he confirmed grimly.

'And she's still trying to contact you after all this time?'

'We still do the occasional private job for them, okay?' Rogan told her. 'Maybe one or two a year. I was out of the country when your letter arrived, which is why I didn't get here as quickly as I should have.' He shrugged. 'What can I say? The guys enjoy keeping their hand in,' he defended, as Elizabeth gave him a pointed stare.

Her brows rose. 'The *guys* do…?'

'Okay, I do too,' he accepted dryly. 'But now we do it on our terms, at our convenience, no one else's, and we gather our own intel,' he explained.

Elizabeth moistened dry lips. 'What sort of jobs?'

'Usually kidnappings and hostage situations that are

too sensitive even for Langley to handle. Satisfied?' he wanted to know.

Elizabeth was far from satisfied, and felt a deep fluttering of unease in the pit of her stomach just at the thought of Rogan putting himself and his men in danger in that way.

Except…

Her mother, instead of accepting the man she was married to as he was, perhaps becoming involved in the things he did and going with him when he travelled on business, had instead tried to change him, to make him into the sort of man she wanted: a stay-at-home husband who worshipped dutifully at her feet. The sort of man Leonard Brown could never hope to be.

That was another thing Elizabeth had learnt today: people could change themselves if they wished to, but another person never could, or should, try to do that changing for them.

Rogan was the man that he was, danger included.

In fact, he was danger with a capital D!

And Elizabeth loved him so much she ached with it!

Rogan watched the changing expressions on Elizabeth's face. The shock at learning what he did. The unease. The trepidation. Was there slight distaste there too…?

'Still think I'm not really a bad-ass?' he mocked, pushing his plate of food away half eaten.

What the hell had he been thinking, making love to this woman? Dragging a woman like Elizabeth Brown—smart, sassy, so courageous and very much the lady—into the low-life world he was occasionally forced to inhabit? He had to have been out of his stupid mind!

He stood up abruptly.

'Where are you going?' Elizabeth demanded sternly as she also stood up.

Rogan raised an eyebrow. 'Well, somewhere in my decision to drive to Surrey with you I forgot that I was going to need transport back to Cornwall. As it's too late now to get a train back, I thought I might look for a hotel to stay in tonight.'

'You can stay here.'

He smiled humourlessly. 'I don't think so, Elizabeth.'

Her chin rose challengingly. 'Why not?'

Why not? Because if Rogan stayed here there was no way he was going to remain on the couch Elizabeth would no doubt consign him to. Not with her in bed only feet away…!

His mouth thinned. 'To answer your earlier question, about giving your father money—'

'I totally agree with you. If I did that it would unbalance the life he and Cheryl now have together,' Elizabeth put in.

Rogan's eyes widened. 'How did you know I was going to say that?'

'The same way you know that the two of us are going to be sharing my bed in just a few minutes,' Elizabeth answered matter-of-factly. 'I know you, Rogan,' she continued, as his expression darkened thunderously. 'For instance, I know that right now you just want to get out of here. Away from me. Away from any temptation to go to bed with me again.'

He folded his muscled arms across the broadness of his chest as he regarded her closely. 'Think a lot of yourself, don't you,' he taunted.

'No. No, I really don't,' Elizabeth said shakily. 'I know you want me. But I have no idea what else you do or don't feel for me. And it doesn't matter.' She gave a rueful shake of her head as she stepped closer to him. 'It's enough for the moment that you want me. And that I want you,' she added softly.

Dear God, Rogan groaned inwardly. No woman should have such deep, mesmerising blue eyes. Or such a poutingly sensual mouth that begged to be kissed. And she certainly shouldn't have the sort of toned and curvaceous body that a man would kill to possess.

That *he* would kill to possess just once more!

He closed the distance between them, his arms moving about her waist like steel bands as he pulled her into him and his mouth fiercely claimed hers.

He was hungry for her. Ravenous. Needed her, wanted her, with the same desperation a drug addict needed his fix.

Even as he devoured her mouth he was curving her body into his, loving the way she fitted so perfectly against him, and his hands were everywhere as he touched her back, her breasts, her hips, finally cupping her bottom to pull her into the hardness of his thighs, groaning as the softness of her curves cupped and held him there.

He kept her that way as he broke the kiss to rest his forehead on hers. 'What am I going to do with you, Elizabeth?' he groaned huskily.

'What do you want to do with me?' Her voice was breathless with need for him.

He drew in a harsh breath. 'I want to kidnap you and take you back to America with me. I want to lock the two of us away naked in my apartment and become your sex-slave until you tire of me!'

'And…?' she choked.

He gave a hard laugh as he released her to step back. 'And you would probably run screaming if I even attempted to so much as take you out of here.'

Elizabeth faced him unflinchingly. 'Try me.'

'Elizabeth—'

'Try me...Rogue.' She deliberately used the name she knew he preferred. She was fighting for what she wanted and she would use any means within her power to get him. Maybe only for a week. Or a month. But what a week or month it would be!

His throat moved as he swallowed before answering her. 'What if there's a condition to taking you back to America with me?'

She eyed him warily. 'What sort of condition?'

'One you're not going to like very much,' he said.

'What's your condition, Rogue?' Elizabeth asked. 'I guarantee in advance that I'll agree to it.'

'The sex was that good, hmm?' he teased.

'For me, the sex was fantastic,' she came back without hesitation.

'Me too,' he admitted huskily.

'Thank you for that.' She smiled. 'But I feel more for you than that, Rogan.'

His lids narrowed. 'How much more?'

'A lot more.'

'Enough to marry me?'

'Enough to—?' Elizabeth stared at him, searching the darkness of his eyes, the grim set of his mouth, the rigidity of his jaw, for any sign that he was teasing her. He wasn't. 'You don't have to marry me, Rogan.'

'I know I don't *have* to marry you!' he exclaimed. 'I don't have to marry anyone. Least of all the Britten heiress!'

'I'll give the money away,' she vowed.

'I couldn't care less what you do with your money, Elizabeth. Keep it. Give it away. Put it in trust for our kids—'

'Our *kids*?' Elizabeth squeaked, incredulous, but delighted that he wanted children with her.

'Kids.' Rogan nodded determinedly. 'I'm sure between the two of us we could do a better job of parenting than our own parents did.'

Elizabeth was sure they could too. 'I'd like that, Rogan.'

He grinned teasingly. 'The trying for them or the having them?'

'Both!'

Rogan chuckled. 'Me too. As for your money… Elizabeth, even before my father died and left me everything I'd earned more than enough these last five years to keep the two of us, and anyone else who comes along, for the rest of our lives.'

Elizabeth looked up at him quizzically. 'Then why were you so angry when you realised who I was?'

'I wasn't angry, I was… It's a male thing, I guess.' He shrugged uncomfortably. 'Not only are you extremely successful in your chosen field, but you're rich as Croesus, too! What could I possibly have to offer that you would want?'

'*You!*' she assured him vehemently. 'I just want you, Rogan,' she repeated more softly.

'I've wanted you since the first night we met,' he admitted honestly.

Her eyes were wide. 'You have?'

'Yeah,' he acknowledged. 'You crawled under my skin

then, Elizabeth Brown, and I can't shake you off. Hell, I don't *want* to shake you off. I even went to Surrey with you today to see your father because I couldn't bear the thought that you'd leave and I'd never see you again. Never be with you again. But God knows what a tutor of history is going to find to do in America…'

'I have absolutely no doubts that the Britten heiress could donate an obscenely large amount of money to one of the colleges in Washington and secure herself a place on the faculty at the same time.' Elizabeth quickly disposed of that particular problem, her heart thundering wildly in her chest. 'I think a more pressing question might be what is Rogue Sullivan going to do with a wife?'

'Oh, that's easy,' Rogan said, with the sexy smile she loved so much. 'I'm going to love her for the rest of our lives, of course.'

Elizabeth swallowed hard, that wild thundering of her heart ceasing abruptly as her breath arrested in her throat. 'You love me?' she finally said haltingly.

'I'd better—or what's the point of marrying you?'

'Rogan, please!'

Rogan closed his eyes briefly, knowing he was making a complete hash of this. But he had never done this before. He was never going to do it again, either! He would either have the courageous, the loyal, the strong, the kind and caring, the lovingly perfect Elizabeth as his wife, or no woman at all.

He opened his eyes, drawing in a deep breath before speaking gruffly. 'I never wanted to fall in love. Didn't believe that I ever would. But I knew I was in trouble that very first night when you attacked me.'

'I thought you were a burglar!' she excused, with an embarrassed laugh.

'Even more reason for me to admire you,' Rogan assured her. 'I can't think of too many women who would have tried to attack a burglar single-handed. You then proceeded, despite your fractured relationship with your own father, to upbraid me for my behaviour towards mine. Criticised my way of life. The way I dress. Just about everything about me, in fact,' he recalled ruefully. 'But then you made love with me like a wildcat!'

'Rogan!' Elizabeth gasped, and the colour deepened in her cheeks.

'Oh, believe me, Beth, I loved it,' he told her huskily. 'I loved every moment of it. So much so that I hope you'll make love with me like that every night for the rest of our lives. So there you have it.' He grimaced at this complete baring of his soul. 'I love you very much, Elizabeth Brown. Will you please marry me, come back to Washington with me, and spend the rest of your life at my side?'

Those blue eyes blazed with emotion, and a becoming blush coloured her cheeks.

Elizabeth knew that they were an oddly matched pair. A woman who had chosen to immerse herself in academia for most of her adult life and an ex-military man, who still dressed like a commando and who, by choice, still lived on the edge of danger some of the time.

Yes, on the surface they were an oddly matched pair. But inside, where it really mattered, Elizabeth knew they fitted together perfectly…

'Oh, yes, Rogan Sullivan, I'll marry you,' she told him happily. 'I'll marry you because I love you very much too!'

She launched herself into his arms, laughing and crying at the same time.

Rogan kissed her very thoroughly, before picking her up and carrying her out of the kitchen and through to her bedroom. He placed her down on the bed and then lay beside her. Reaching up, he cupped either side of his face with his hands and looked down at her with intense dark eyes. 'I promise that my love for you will last for ever, Beth.'

'For ever sounds perfect, Rogue.'

For ever with Rogan was absolutely all that Elizabeth could ever want or need…

0410/02/MB276

## millsandboon.co.uk Community

# *Join Us!*

The Community is the perfect place to meet and chat to kindred spirits who love books and reading as much as you do, but it's also the place to:

- **Get the inside scoop from authors about their latest books**
- **Learn how to write a romance book with advice from our editors**
- **Help us to continue publishing the best in women's fiction**
- **Share your thoughts on the books we publish**
- **Befriend other users**

**Forums:** Interact with each other as well as authors, editors and a whole host of other users worldwide.

**Blogs:** Every registered community member has their own blog to tell the world what they're up to and what's on their mind.

**Book Challenge:** We're aiming to read 5,000 books and have joined forces with The Reading Agency in our inaugural Book Challenge.

**Profile Page:** Showcase yourself and keep a record of your recent community activity.

**Social Networking:** We've added buttons at the end of every post to share via digg, Facebook, Google, Yahoo, technorati and de.licio.us.

*www.millsandboon.co.uk*

0310_P0ZED

# 2 FREE BOOKS
## AND A SURPRISE GIFT

We would like to take this opportunity to thank you for reading this Mills & Boon® book by offering you the chance to take TWO more specially selected books from the Modern™ series absolutely FREE! We're also making this offer to introduce you to the benefits of the Mills & Boon® Book Club™—

- **FREE home delivery**
- **FREE gifts and competitions**
- **FREE monthly Newsletter**
- **Exclusive Mills & Boon Book Club offers**
- **Books available before they're in the shops**

Accepting these FREE books and gift places you under no obligation to buy, you may cancel at any time, even after receiving your free books. Simply complete your details below and return the entire page to the address below. You don't even need a stamp!

**YES** Please send me 2 free Modern books and a surprise gift. I understand that unless you hear from me, I will receive 4 superb new books every month for just £3.19 each, postage and packing free. I am under no obligation to purchase any books and may cancel my subscription at any time. The free books and gift will be mine to keep in any case.

Ms/Mrs/Miss/Mr______________ Initials ______________

Surname ____________________________

Address ____________________________

____________________ Postcode __________

Send this whole page to: Mills & Boon Book Club, Free Book Offer, FREEPOST NAT 10298, Richmond, TW9 1BR

Offer valid in UK only and is not available to current Mills & Boon Book Club subscribers to this series. Overseas and Eire please write for details.. We reserve the right to refuse an application and applicants must be aged 18 years or over. Only one application per household. Terms and prices subject to change without notice. Offer expires 31st May 2010. As a result of this application, you may receive offers from Harlequin Mills & Boon and other carefully selected companies. If you would prefer not to share in this opportunity please write to The Data Manager, PO Box 676, Richmond, TW9 1WU.